LITTLE,
BROWN

1837

LARGE
PRINT

Girls in Trucks

Katie Crouch

LITTLE, BROWN AND COMPANY

Little, Brown and Company
Hachette Book Group USA
237 Park Avenue, New York, NY 10017
Visit our Web site at www.HachetteBookGroupUSA.com

First Large Print Edition: April 2008
The Large Print Edition published in accord with the
standards of the N.A.V.H.

The author gratefully acknowledges the editors of the
Washington Square Review, where "Sleeping with Dogs"
was published in an earlier form, and the editors of the
Charleston Post and Courier, where "Bitsy's List"
was published in an earlier form as a South Carolina
Fiction Project winner.

ISBN 978-0-316-02761-8
LCCN 2007938290

10 9 8 7 6 5 4 3 2 1

RRD-IN

Book design by Brooke Koven

Printed in the United States of America

For Mom—
mother, scientist, role model, friend,
and decidedly
not Camellia material.

CONTENTS

Girls in Trucks

A DEBUTANTE'S CODE TO DYING

IF YOU ARE WHITE, are a girl or boy between the ages of nine and twelve, and, according to a certain committee of mothers, are good enough to associate with Charleston's other good girls and boys, then Wednesday night is a busy night for you. Wednesday night, from four until seven in the evening, is reserved for Cotillion Training School, or, as it is called casually among the students and their families, dancing school. The number of students is severely limited. Due to demand, children are usually signed up shortly after they are born.

The mainstay of the school is the Fox Trot, although other, more modern dances are also taught after the classics have been learned. The Lindy Hop. The Cha-Cha. The Shag is not taught, as, according to Miss Taylor, the school's headmistress, it is common. But naturally, dancing is not all the children learn at Cotillion Training School. At Miss Taylor's school, children are trained how to greet adults properly, how to receive refreshments gracefully, and how not to eat everything on their plate. In a society that is doing its best to leave formality behind, *this* program works to undo modern attitudes of brashness, to teach children manners, to arm students with the social tools they will need throughout their adult lives!

My name is Sarah Walters, and what I knew was that Cotillion meant sweat. It meant sticky thighs in saggy stockings. It meant soupy nights in the South Carolina Society Hall, where you were required to wear white gloves. My mother told me that I was wearing the gloves to show I was a lady, but after the first dance, I realized that the gloves also were about perspiration, as they instantly became soaked from the wet palms of boys as we step-ball-stepped to the tinny record player.

I went to Cotillion Training School for the same reason my friends went: my mother wanted me to. This was important to her, the same way it was important to have a picture of her great-great-grandfather dressed in Confederate gray over the sideboard and for us not to be seen in Dad's truck when we were in town. She is a member of the Camellia Society, founded in the 1820s by some Charleston ladies. You have to be born into it to be a member. The main purpose of the club was originally musical enjoyment, but after a few years the Camellias gave up that pretense and stood behind what it really was: an organization whose purpose was to gather, socialize with people of similar interests, and—most important—prepare their daughters for marriage to a decent man.

I never understood the Camellia Society, really. I went to the meetings and I ate the cake. I listened to the lectures given by the Mama Camellias on various topics: the importance of a consistently neat appearance, why one must not be seen out socially too often, the tastefulness of floral arrangements, how to sit properly in a chair. And, if the words themselves seemed silly, the weight they were given by the women in the room earned our respectful silence. We knew that as long as we listened, we were Camellias, and as long as we were Camellias, we were protected. The only question left unanswered was, from what?

Girls, at Cotillion Training School, you will learn the following:
> *The Waltz*
> *The Fox Trot*
> *The Lindy Hop*
> *The Rumba*
> *The Cha-Cha*

Girls, you will not, under any circumstances, be taught the Shag. Don't ask about the Shag. The Shag is a common dance. You don't Shag now, you won't Shag later. Accept it. Live with it. Now go on, put on those white gloves and smile.

People say that Charleston's social structure is complex, but really, everything can pretty much be explained by the fourth-grade Cotillion line.

The future debutantes, the ones with balls already planned for certain years, stood in front. The Camellias were one of the oldest societies, so we were first. Behind us were the Magnolias (as old as us but not as famous), the Stonelochs (secretive, a little weird), and the Cotillion Society (only two generations old, so not really taken seriously yet). The next layer of the line was made up of girls whose parents had been in Charleston for a while—a generation or two—but who weren't going to be debutantes. Maybe their parents were liberal, or perhaps their father had married someone from out of state. Those girls usually stood in the middle and appeared comfortable and happy, but a little confused about why they were there.

Then there were the new money girls. I felt most sorry for them. These were daughters of parents who had recently moved to Charleston and who were trying to buy their way in. You could tell the new money girls from us by their clothes. Girls who belonged wore hand-me-downs from other debs, sisters, or family friends. New money girls had new dresses just for Cotillion. Sometimes, if their mothers were truly clueless, they had lace gloves. Girls with lace gloves received no mercy. Miss Taylor would glare at their hands disapprovingly; the other girls would stare and giggle. Plus, they were definitely, for the rest of the year and probably forever, going to be stuck at the back of the line.

I didn't mind Cotillion Training School too much. It was fun to go to the city on a weeknight to hang out with Bitsy, Charlotte, and Annie. Charlotte—wild and inappropriate, the daughter of divorced parents—was the only one I really liked, but we were all Camellias, so we formed a sort of alliance. Each Wednesday night, before letting me out of the car, my mother would look me over sharply, spit on her finger, and rub my cheeks. Then she'd leave, and the Camellias and I would link arms and climb the marble steps of the dance hall together. We'd stand in line across from the boys, giggling, whispering, and twitching nervously at what was ahead: the inevitable moment when we'd have to release one another, reach out across the room, and ask, cheeks on fire, to be touched.

Girls, let's talk about boys. I know this is a confusing time for all of you. You may have strange feelings. You may sense funny things happening to your body. We all know, for instance, that Annie is getting a little bigger around the chest already. We can speak privately about that, one-on-one. I have a pamphlet. You see, you are blooming, and it makes the boys act silly. They are like bees, buzzing around you, and it is your job not to taunt them, girls. Do not taunt the bees, girls. Do not taunt the bees.

At Cotillion Training School, you were not allowed to dance with your cousin. It was a rule, the same way it was a rule that you had to wear gloves, and that the boys moved clockwise in the dance circle, and that you had to look the chaperones in the eye when you told them good night. Miss Taylor explained that it was unnatural to dance with your cousin, or brother, or anyone in your family before you were sixteen.

"What is she afraid of?" Bitsy asked me. "I like dancing with my brother." Bitsy's older brother was a star dancer. At her house, they danced all the time. He'd whirl her around,

doing advanced steps, even lifting her in the air
sometimes and flipping her over his head. He
had graduated from Cotillion already but still
got paid ten dollars each Wednesday to assist
Miss Taylor with class.

"She thinks that y'all will hump," Charlotte
said. "In the Ladies' Lounge."

"That's perverted," Bitsy said, shuddering
slightly. "You're *perverted*."

Personally, I liked this rule. I didn't have a
brother, but I did have a cousin, and I wouldn't
have danced with him anyway, not if you'd
zapped me in a thunderstorm with an electric
cattle prod.

Ted Wheeler was my mother's first cousin's
son. When we were little, we played together.
There is a picture of us on the beach, and
another one of us naked with a flock of yellow plastic ducks in a tub. Ted was a very good
dancer and won the silver dollar for Fox Trotter
of the Year three times. Bitsy and Annie were a
little in awe of him. It was only a dollar, but still,
it was a big deal, honorwise.

"Do you think Ted would pick me as his partner at Cotillion graduation?" Bitsy asked one

night while we hung out on the stairs, waiting for my mother. "I really want a silver dollar."

"Sure," I said. Bitsy was pretty. She was probably the prettiest girl in dancing school, with silky hair that never got messy, even at a slumber party, and huge blue eyes. Annie and Charlotte were pretty too, but Charlotte was dark, and Annie was fat—she already had breasts as big as my mother's, and her arms swelled sweetly against the elastic puffed sleeves of her dresses. As for me, I coasted by. I wasn't too fat or too thin. I had braces and freckles and straight brown hair that crackled with electricity in a way that I liked when I brushed it in winter. Still, next to Bitsy, I was nothing. So of course Ted Wheeler would dance with Bitsy. It was sort of silly that she was even asking the question. Not that I approved, though; Ted Wheeler was no one that Bitsy should want to dance with. I knew that she could take care of herself, but Ted was mean. His soul was as black as summer tar.

"You don't want to dance with Ted, Bitsy," I said. "He's evil."

Bitsy shrugged. "I guess. He seems OK."

She was wrong, though. After that tub picture

was snapped, Ted Wheeler tried to drown me. Once, I had to get stitches because he hit me on the head with a Tonka Truck. Ted's father had left Cousin Cindy for a lady who wore tennis skirts, but it was my opinion that he probably also left because of Ted Wheeler. Ted was bad, even when he was a baby, and by the time we got to Cotillion Training School, he was worse. He brought in a BB gun and shot the girl with Down syndrome. He called the kid with the birthmark Freak Face. Me, he hated the most. He pinched me and punched me and told me I was ugly. One night, right in front of everyone, he shoved me down the grand stairway, and when I hit bottom, bruised and breathless, he ran down after me and pulled my hair while pretending to help me up.

"You're ugly," he hissed in my ear.

"I hate you," I said back. I told everyone that I hated Ted. Bitsy, Annie, my teachers, my parents.

"You cannot hate Ted Wheeler," my mother said patiently. "He is my cousin Cindy's son."

"But I do," I said. I didn't like the way these feelings made me act, but the fact was, Ted

Wheeler was horrible and I hated him. I knew I was right. It was my own personal constant. Another rule to live by.

Step-ball-step
Step-ball-step
SHIFT WEIGHT
Step-ball-step
Step-ball-step
SHIFT WEIGHT

From what I could tell, the boys did not have the same silent rules about lining up as we did. They stood together in a huffing, snorting jumble, popping Chinese noisemakers and, on more hectic nights, setting off smoke bombs. After the first few Wednesdays, I didn't spend time trying to understand who on the boys' side sat where. In grade school, boys are not something to analyze. They are, as a collective, a thing to be survived.

A few weeks after Ted Wheeler threw me down the stairs, though, it finally became clear that I had to fight back. It wasn't about just me anymore. This time, he went for Annie.

It was raining that Wednesday. Rainy nights at Cotillion Training School are especially unpleasant, because your hair frizzes and the already hot hallway is blanketed in a swampy adolescent haze. Charlotte — whom Ted also hated but also slightly feared — was sick that night, leaving us open for an attack. It was hot, so Annie's face was particularly flushed. A little line of sweat trickled down her cheek. Ted made his way over through the crowd. I had developed a radar for Ted as a self-protection device practically since birth, so I saw him coming right away. Instinctively, I hunched my shoulders.

Ted smiled at me sweetly, so I relaxed a little. It seemed that he wasn't aiming for me. Maybe he was coming to talk to Bitsy? That would make sense, because all the boys did. She must have thought the same because she smiled, cocking her head expectantly, then frowned in confusion as Ted passed her and proceeded to sink his finger deep into Annie's plentiful stomach flesh.

"Moooo!" Ted yelled, causing the crowd around us to titter nervously. Even Bitsy giggled for a second. "The cow says moooooooo."

I looked at Annie's face, which was red with horror.

"Shut up, Ted," I said, shoving him. He shoved me back harder, then walked away, still laughing. Annie's eyes were brimming with tears.

"I can't help it," she said. "I even did the Jane Fonda video today."

Bitsy and I were quiet. I was too angry to talk, and Bitsy was not great at talking during times like these. Still, through the first half of class, I plotted. I waited until the lesson was half over, then I pulled Bitsy aside in the brownie-and-cola line.

"You know what?" I whispered to her. "Ted Wheeler has three nipples."

Bitsy's eyes widened. She loved secrets and could be relied upon to keep them for about two minutes. "Really?" she asked.

"Yes," I said. "And one time, I saw Ted Wheeler hump his own cat."

"That's so perverted!" she said. "What kind of cat?"

"White," I said, my mind racing wildly. "Its name was Mittens."

"I don't believe you," Bitsy said, looking over at Ted.

"I'm his cousin," I said. "I know."

In the time it took to consume three brownies and a Sprite, Bitsy had asked Ted about his third nipple. He stared at me from across the waxed dance floor, eyes narrowed. Recalling the pain of my head smacking against the stairs, I felt the fearful urge to vomit. But he said nothing to me, and when class ended, I smiled at Annie and made my way to the coat line.

There, in the unsupervised vacuum that was the dark, dusty place behind the stairs, Ted Wheeler and three other boys grabbed me. They pulled me into an even darker corner and held me down as I fought. Bitsy and Annie were already outside, but other girls were watching—I remember shiny blue and yellow dresses scattering like crows in buckshot. Bitsy's brother put his hand over my mouth. Ted Wheeler shoved his hand up my dress. He yanked at my tights and pulled my dress up. They had covered my eyes, but I could hear laughing, could feel groping and poking by something cold.

"She's so ugly," Ted Wheeler said. "She smells like a dog."

I fought. I kicked. I scratched. I bit, smelled chicken, tasted flesh. Someone yelped in pain, and they let me up, and I heard a clatter, saw a Sprite bottle roll across the floor.

I stood up and smoothed my dress down. Bitsy's brother's hand was bleeding. I didn't cry, but still, something was flooding in me.

"You're going to die, Ted Wheeler," I said.

A flash of fear crossed Ted Wheeler's face, quick as a mullet. The other boys backed away. Bitsy's brother ran.

"That's right," I said. "Ted Wheeler, you're going to die and burn in hell."

He stared at me for a moment before doubling over cruelly into a laugh. Then, Ted Wheeler drew his head back and spat on me.

Cotillion Training School ends in seventh grade. Our debutante ball isn't until after high school, so for the in-between years, you sort of forget you're a Camellia. There's no more Fox

Trotting, and other than a committee meeting at Christmas, the Mama Camellias leave you alone.

The Camellias parted ways after dancing school. Charlotte and I stayed best friends, but Bitsy, Annie, and I drifted apart once the Cotillion glue loosened. The same social hierarchy no longer seemed to apply; instead of family status, popularity was based on traditional factors, like looks and sports skills. We were still Camellia sisters, but Bitsy didn't always like to be seen with people like Annie and Charlotte and me. She now existed in the unattainable girl-with-older-surfer-boyfriends group, while Charlotte hung with the stoners and Annie got fatter and sank into the giggly choir-girl circle. I spent most of my time in the school newspaper office. While I couldn't control anything that went on with boys or who liked me at school, I could at least report on them in the "anonymous" weekly social column, and when feeling especially powerful, I could put my name next to protests of burning injustices, such as the lack of vegetarian options in the cafeteria. This was not seen as particularly cool by anyone except

Charlotte and the few pale boys I was friends with. Still, I had a place to go at lunch, which, in high school, is pretty much all you need.

Ted Wheeler went away to boarding school, so I barely ever had to see him. My mother didn't do much with Cousin Cindy anyway. Cindy had turned into a sort of sad cousin, living in her big alimony house on Broad Street. She had been lovely when she was married to Ted's dad, but now, my mother observed, she was getting dumpy. It is the duty of the Camellia to observe. She does not insult directly, but instead sandwiches her blows between compliments drizzled in honey.

"Cindy has the prettiest hair," my mother would say. *"A little too fond of the bacon bits,* but goodness, that hair is shiny."

"Cindy has the nicest disposition. *Bottom the size of a lumber barge,* but the nicest manners you can find."

In what I considered a divine example of universal justice, Ted Wheeler had grown up ugly. He was too skinny and had a big nose and an inexplicably thick neck. My mother called him "awkward." One night, at a summer party in a red clay field, I even felt sort of sorry for Ted Wheeler. He came alone and sat on his car by himself. I was smoking a cigarette with Bitsy in an attempt to fit in somewhere for a few minutes, but when she turned to her surfer boyfriend and started kissing him, I decided to go over, why not, say hello.

"Hi, Ted," I said.

He looked at me with the brown, flat discs that were his eyes.

"Hey, it's soda cunt," Ted Wheeler said. "Had any Sprite lately?"

I turned and went back to Bitsy. She looked at my face and untangled herself momentarily from her boyfriend.

"What is it?" she said.

"Ted Wheeler," I said. The old fear was back. "He called me a cunt."

Bitsy's mouth dropped open to form a perfect, pretty *O*. She turned to her boyfriend. "Oh, my God. Sarah's cousin is a total dick."

"Really?" the boyfriend said.

I bit back the tears. I felt safer next to Bitsy and her boyfriend. Even though they almost always ignored me in public, the surfer was looking at me with interest. I sensed a fleeting moment of chance. Bitsy watched me patiently, waiting for me to talk.

"He has three nipples," I said.

"No way." The surfer looked at Ted and cackled. Bitsy laughed too.

I saw Ted Wheeler turn red. He seemed scared, and God help me, I wasn't even a little bit sorry.

"It's true," I said. "He masturbates four times a day." There was a group forming now of older people who never talked to me. Ted got up and opened the door of his car. I felt a rush as I talked, even as I watched him drive away.

"He screws his own socks! And once—and this is true, y'all, I saw it—Ted Wheeler, he pulled down his pants and screwed his own stupid cat."

Girls, let's talk about the months before the ball. This is, as you know, a crucial time, girls. Crucial. Refrain from any drastic beauty decisions within a year before the event—meaning hair color, length. I don't even want to talk about last year's nose-ring incident. Also, girls—Annie, listen up here!—please watch your figure during those first few months of college. I know about

the sweets in the sorority houses, but stick to the celery
sticks, girls. You'll be so glad when you step into that
white dress and it fits you, just like a glove!

Ted Wheeler did not come to my ball. He was
invited because he was my cousin, but then his
head got smashed in.

Your actual ball takes place during the first
year of college. At the time of my coming out,
I was, frankly, not very concerned about the
Camellias. They were far away at state schools
with sorority houses that looked like castles,
while I ended up at a small liberal arts college in
upstate New York, where I learned to smoke pot
and studied writing under a man who wore a top
hat to class. I gave my mother a list of friends I
wanted to invite and left the rest of the arrangements to her and all the other Mama Camellias. Still, the month before the event, I got calls
almost every day about guest lists and flowers
and relative quantities of shrimp. There were
daily emergencies on the answering machine:
Bitsy's mother was trying to cut off the liquor
at eleven, and the Elliotts were inviting the
Rubensteins — can you *imagine?*

On a Thursday night a week before the ball, my roommate handed me the phone and then sat next to me on my bunk. We were drinking wine coolers and studying for our history final.

"Darling."

"Mom."

My mother didn't answer, and I heard her blow her nose on the other end of the line. I looked at my roommate nervously. She got up off the bed and handed me a bong.

"What?" I asked.

"Ted Wheeler can't come to your debutante ball."

"What?"

"Ted Wheeler."

I took a hit and blinked, confused.

"I hate Ted Wheeler."

"Yes, well."

"All right. So he can't come. There'll be lots of nice boys there, Mom. Don't worry about it."

My roommate rolled her eyes and took the bong back.

"Oh, dear. No, I mean he can't come because he's been in a car accident, honey. Something about a midnight trip to Sweet Briar."

I couldn't process this information. It seemed too much like a soap opera. I felt the urge to laugh.

"What?" I said, and she repeated herself, told me again about the accident. Ted Wheeler had been unconscious for three days. Another boy had died.

"Will Ted die?" I asked. My words hung in the air, and I turned away, as if they were visible.

"I don't know." She blew her nose. "Oh, dear. I hope this doesn't ruin the party. Oh, God, I can't believe I just said that."

"Where is he?"

"Why?"

"I don't know," I said, because I didn't.

"He's in Hampton Memorial Hospital. Send a card, will you? That would really be very polite."

I said that I would. I said that it would be OK, that the flowers she had picked for the stage would be pretty, that everyone would love the artichoke dip. Then I hung up, borrowed my roommate's car, and drove down to Hampton,

Virginia. I don't remember how long it took; when I got there, night was almost gone.

When Camellias visit someone in the hospital, they usually bring something savory. Everyone brings sugar, the Mama Camellias say. What people in tragedy need is salt.

I didn't bring anything with me to Hampton. I thought about picking up some french fries, but they would have been cold by the time I arrived. It was late when I finally got to Ted's hospital. I sat in the parking lot for about an hour, smoking the cigarettes I found in the glove compartment. At dawn I got out of the car. I brushed my hair, popped a piece of gum, and walked tentatively into the lobby. Ted Wheeler's room, according to the pinch-faced woman at the information desk, was 412. There was a window of plate glass in the door, and through it I could see Ted Wheeler lying on a twin bed, connected to an octopus of tubes. His room was filled with flowers, and cards, and a huge painted banner that read, *Ted—Virginia Tech Loves You—You Rock!* It was signed by hundreds of people. No one was in the room with Ted.

I went in. Ted Wheeler was naked under the sheet. I could see the outline of his legs. The left side of his face was red, purple, gooey, like the inside of a pulpy plum.

I went closer. I blew on his nose.

"Hey," I said.

Ted Wheeler did not wake up.

"Ted," I said.

Not a wince.

I stood there for a while—a minute? an hour?—until I heard Cousin Cindy's voice. I quickly darted out of the room and took the side stairs back down to the parking lot, then drove back to school and took my history exam.

> *Camellias, Camellias*
> *Pink, rose, and white*
> *The most beautiful flower*
> *To bloom in the Southern night!*
> *Strong of root*
> *And beautiful of bloom*
> *Once you are out*
> *You are sure to find a groom!*

The Camellia debutante ball takes place the night before Christmas Eve during the freshman holiday season. Everyone was home, so the phone was constantly ringing, and my house was buzzing with fragile, intoxicating excitement. It was fun seeing the girls again. I'd gone the farthest away for school, so I was the most exotic for at least ten minutes. Then Bitsy announced that she had had an abortion, and the attention turned back to her, where it probably belonged.

Camellias dress together for the party. It's a tradition. Bitsy's house was closest to the dance hall, so we all went there and set up in what once was a small ballroom, our mothers toting toolboxes of makeup and hot rollers, our fathers following, sheepishly holding our mothers' old wedding gowns. The Camellia mothers had hired a hair lady, and a nail lady, and two other black ladies to clean up our mess. We spent six hours getting our hair poufed and eating tea sandwiches, except for Annie, who wasn't eating anything but Slim-Fast. At five, the Camellia mothers let us have champagne, and the parents cleared out to go home, have a real drink, and get themselves spiffed up.

Bitsy's brother came in during the downtime and told us we looked hot. "All these future brides," he said. "Which one should I marry?" He gave us all hits out of a Coke can, which was too bad for Bitsy, who couldn't handle her pot. She spent the rest of beauty time staring at her teeth in the mirror. It didn't matter—she was still the prettiest anyway. The rest of the Camellias sat in a circle, staring at one another, talking about, what else, Ted Wheeler.

"I heard he was a total vegetable," Charlotte said.

"Will he be OK?" Annie asked.

"I know Ted Wheeler," Bitsy's brother said. "He's an awesome guy."

"But you don't like him, right?" Bitsy asked me.

"He's in a *coma*," Annie said, as if that was my answer. I shrugged. Bitsy's brother gave me another hit. Annie went into the bathroom to vomit. It was time to go.

Our Camellia ball was the best in years, people said. The shrimp sculpture was especially fabulous. My mother was glowing. There was even a good story to tell over breakfast, because Bitsy's brother ripped the top off Charlotte's dress on the dance floor. She had made her dress herself, and when it tore, momentarily showing half a nipple, she slapped him and left. Still, everyone I talked to agreed it hadn't been Bitsy's brother's fault. Boys will be boys, my father said, and who wore a revealing dress like that to a dance, anyway? It wasn't ladylike, a dress like that.

Cousin Cindy was not at the ball. Word had it she was spending Christmas in Virginia at the hospital. Mom was still worried that the Ted Wheeler incident would ruin the evening, but people in Charleston are very serious about parties. Besides, really, Ted wasn't missed by many. Aside from a few pitying murmurs and nods by the bar, no one talked about Ted Wheeler at all.

Girls, after the ball, you may feel a little depressed, due to a phenomenon called the "postseason blues." This is completely understandable. After all, the debutante tradition was started in order to present girls of a certain social class to men of a certain social class for marriage, but these days, no eighteen-year-olds actually get married, do they? But don't fret, girls. Go forth knowing that you will always shine just a little bit brighter than other girls, that you will always be just a tad more graceful. Once a Camellia, always a Camellia, girls. Now, tomorrow, forever.

It got sad, having a cousin in a coma.

I would be lying if I said my freshman year centered around Ted Wheeler, but I did think about him sometimes. I should take good notes in this class, I'd think, because Ted's missing freshman English. I should get a tape of this concert and give it to Ted when he wakes up.

I still hated him, of course. It wasn't like anything he'd ever done was suddenly OK. Still, he might be nicer when he woke up. He might have amnesia. Maybe then we could be friends.

Sometimes, when I drank too much, I'd talk about it to a certain willing boy named Brett.

"I saw him," I told Brett. "I went down there in the middle of the night just to make myself believe it."

"Crazy," Brett said, fingering a belt loop on my jeans.

"I hate him, though," I said. "Once, when we were little, he even tried to kill me."

"That's terrible," Brett said. "Dude. That's really screwed up."

"But then I told him I wanted him dead. I guess I *did* want him dead. But now…what do you think? Do you think that's bad? Do you think I'm going to hell?"

"Well," Brett said thoughtfully, "only if he dies."

It took Ted Wheeler eight months and three days to die.

Actually, it took Cousin Cindy that long to give up on him. Which, everyone said, was understandable, under the circumstances.

In Charleston, funerals are well attended, especially if the person is young and from a good family. St. Michael's Church on Meeting and Broad can seat three hundred, and it was packed. Camellias do not wear black to funerals, so my mother had me wear a blue sundress with a sweater to cover my shoulders. Bitsy came in dusky pink.

My mother put herself in charge of the reception, directing the other mothers where to put the hams, the turkeys, the great dishes of crab dip. She is very good at funerals. She knows

exactly what to make (spinach-and-feta casserole), what supplies to pick up (paper plates and
napkins — funerals are not a time for china), and
what liquor to serve (wine and bourbon: lots).
All of the Mama Camellias were there, though
no one actually talked about Ted's dying. A
Camellia does not cry at a funeral if she can help
it. Her role is to support, not add to the sorrow.

The word at the house was that Cindy was
taking things well. She looked great, my mother
said, considering. Pretty as a picture. *A bit high on
meds,* but calm as a spring day. Still, she looked
sort of bad to me. She sat alone, drinking wine
and staring vacantly at the wall.

"Go say hello to Cousin Cindy," my mother
directed me. I went and sat on the couch.

"Hi, Cindy."

She looked at me blankly. For a moment I
thought maybe she didn't know who I was.

"I'm your cousin," I said.

"I know." She smiled. "Of course I know
that." She sipped her wine while I sat beside her,
silent.

"I should tell you," I said finally, "that I...um.
I should tell you that I went and saw Ted. In the

hospital, I mean. I didn't see you there. But I drove down to see him. We didn't like each other. Did you know that? Actually, we really kind of hated each other. So it was a little weird. But I drove down anyway. I don't know why."

Cindy was staring at a group of mothers huddled in the kitchen. My own mother said something, and they bubbled with laughter. Cindy didn't take her gaze away. I wondered if she'd heard me.

"Ted loved you very much," Cindy said after a few long seconds. "He was a very good boy."

"Yes, ma'am," I said. "Sure. He really was."

Lately, Miss Taylor has become very concerned over the future of Cotillion Training School.

"People just don't do the classic steps anymore," she tells me when she corners me at this year's Camellia ball. "Manners and tradition don't mean anything to these people. Some of the mothers are even asking me to reconsider the Shag."

This is my last debutante ball. Traditionally,

you go see the next round of debs the year after you come out in order to offer your support, and then you sort of move on into the blank space between being a deb and being a Mama Camellia. I am here without an escort, which Miss Taylor disapproves of. She also disapproves of the short dress I've borrowed from my roommate. So far I've spent most of the night in the buffet line with Annie, watching Bitsy do the Lindy. Although I am trying to behave well, I have not been able to look anyone in the eye tonight while greeting them. I have also eaten all the shrimp on my plate.

Before the ball ends, Bitsy's brother asks me to dance. I catch my mother's eye, and she smiles, delighted. He's drunk—so drunk that he calls me the wrong name. I say yes anyway. As we go to the floor, it is announced that this will be the last dance of the night. I request, and am granted, a Fox Trot.

UP AT YALE

MY FAMILY'S HOUSE was built in 1826. We don't know who built it. We tell people that the first inhabitant was an ancestor of my father's, but that could be wrong; all of the historical ledgers of the house were lost when it was occupied by the Union Army, 1864. That really did happen. It's in a history book. People call the house the Point, probably because it's set on a pointed bluff of Johns Island, half an hour outside of town. But then again, there might be other reasons for the name. My father just sort of made up that story, and now the story has become what we know.

The Point used to be a cotton plantation

house. It's not as big as you would think a plantation house would be; in fact, if you came to visit, you wouldn't suspect that there was anything special about it at all, other than its age. There are no columns or indoor bowling alleys or ballrooms. There's a front parlor with pretty furniture where no one goes, and a back den with worn couches and a TV, and a basement full of old bicycles and moldy water toys. My father always believed in as little renovation as possible, so the windows are a million years old; all of the glass is warped, so when you look out, it is like peering down through the top of a flash-frozen stream. When you walk in, you are met with a mysterious but distinct smell, something along the lines of mildew and smoked ham and laundry soap and bourbon. Porches wrap around every corner of the house. In the morning you can face east and see the sun slip in, and at night you can run to the other side to see the marsh drink up the last of the orange-and-pink light.

My father was born in the house, and he filled it in the manner of someone who was created in the place where he resides. His presence stretched into every corner and crevice; he knew how to fix every pipe and tile and board. My mother and I happily curled up in the musty corners with books and stretched out in the hammocks to watch the dog chase raccoons in the grass. All of us loved the Point except for my sister, Eloise. She hated it. As a toddler, she would run away from it, hiding for hours in other people's yards, green plots of fertilized grass with swing sets and swimming pools. She called our house "Yokel Land." From the start, Eloise was on a different team.

My father always said my sister could be anything. She could be a doctor, or a lawyer, or even a famous fashion model. "Anything," he'd repeat, pouring himself a glass of ice-cold gin.

When I was fourteen, Eloise was accepted to Yale. Getting into an Ivy is a big deal in South Carolina. Everyone was proud. My father littered our house with Yale coffee mugs. My mother began wearing accessories marked with little white *Y*s.

Eloise was three years older than me, a senior to my freshman. The day the letter came, she had been out in a johnboat on the river. It was April, but the afternoon hazes of summer had already arrived, softening the sun. I quietly watched her open the thick envelope, listening to the clicking of crabs fighting in the marsh. Eloise's toes were covered in oil-black mud, and salt water dripped from her limbs, smearing the type on the stiff vanilla pages.

"Thank fucking *God*," she said, smiling. "I'm out of here, Tiny. Yale. I *knew* it." A boy waiting on the bleached-out dock called to her—I can't remember who, there were many boys of Eloise—and she handed over the letter and ran out to him.

My sister was the kind of walking oxymoron that doesn't usually exist anywhere but in the movies. The wildest partyer, but valedictorian. The most promiscuous, yet the most respected girl in the class. She understood the nuances of teen politics and sex, and she ruled our private school in Charleston. She planned on being a scientist, or a novelist—president, maybe. There was no doubt in anyone's mind that she was a genius. Her teachers were inspired by her, her friends worshipped her, and my parents were a little in awe of the fact that they had produced something so fine.

It kind of sucked, being Eloise's sister.

My grades were good, but only average good. And unlike Eloise, who inherited my mother's dancer's limbs and shampoo-commercial hair that spread over her shoulders in calm waves, I got stick-straight locks and my father's legs — as in, great for soccer, not so great in short skirts. Plus, remember how the big sisters in movies are always looking out for their siblings at school? That wasn't Eloise. During my first week as a freshman, I brought my sandwich over and sat at her table during lunch. She stiffened visibly and glowered at me.

"Is this your sister?" one of her friends finally asked. I felt the jealous stares of the other girls. Obviously, they would kill just to be related to someone as *totally awesome* as Eloise.

"Yes," Eloise said. "And she's going away now."

The girls laughed. "Just let her eat here to-day," one of them said.

"This is not a charity," Eloise said in a philosophical tone. "This is high school. One must make her own way. Sink or swim." The girls nodded, in awe of her wisdom. "Sorry, Tiny. Go mingle."

I looked around but saw no one I could talk to. So I went to the bathroom, locked myself in a stall, and passed the remainder of lunch eating my peanut butter sandwich in minuscule bites. The rest of freshman year, I skirted her presence, ducking into the bathroom or behind a locker whenever she and her entourage floated down the hall in a cloud of BonneBell lip gloss and Benetton Colors perfume.

Home, though, was separate territory. The rules were different, and Eloise did not ignore me. Instead, she spent her free time ordering me around and describing the sexual bits of her life, as if these details were absolutely crucial to my education.

"Tiny," she called one spring Saturday as I passed by her room. This was her nickname for me. As in, Tiny Tits. "Did I tell you about Jason's penis?"

"No," I said, creeping quietly through the door.

"Go get me a Coke."

I ran to the kitchen and back. When I entered again, she was on the phone. She motioned for me to sit on her beanbag chair while she finished a long talk with one of her friends about whether a bikini top with jean shorts was an appropriate outfit for a keg party. "Sexy," she was saying, "but consider the bug-bite factor. I would advise against." Finally, she hung up and looked at me. "God, these girls are idiots. Anyway," she said, as if she had not just taken a thirty-minute break from our conversation, "Jason's penis."

"Yes."

"It's fucking huge."

I sat back in the spongy plastic of the chair, trying to look nonchalant. Jason, a wiry soccer player, was Eloise's boyfriend of two weeks. I didn't know anything about him other than he was a semisuccessful goalie and his hair was always in his face. "How huge?"

"Approximately the thickness of one of those pickles you get with a club sandwich at

Swensons. We had to use, like, half a container of Vaseline to get it in."

"Oh."

The phone rang again. She stared at me, making sure I understood the magnitude of the situation, and then answered. "Hey." She glanced at me. "Tiny. Go away. Important." So I left, faced with an afternoon that yawned ahead with nothing to do but imagine my sister mounting a giant, lubricated pickle.

I guess in a way I worshipped my sister too. I pretty much clung to her every word. As sophomore year approached, though, I wasn't exactly sorry to see her go. I was sick of just watching and had started to crave some of her high school power for myself. I even helped her pack. She did not think this was strange and seemed to expect it as my inherent duty. "Grab this," she barked. "Fold that." Still, I knew that Eloise loved me, mainly because she took the time to teach me two things: first, she locked us in the bathroom and, using a CoverGirl compact mirror, showed me how to use a tampon. Then, while I was reeling in shock from that exhibition, she taught me how to smoke.

"Breathe in," she said, handing me a lit Camel Light, "and hold." I did and coughed gray. She showed me again, and we shared the cigarette, leaning out her window.

"Are you scared to leave?" I finally asked.

"Of course not." She looked down at the backyard, which had been beaten to yellow-brown by five months of relentless sun. "Tiny. Even the question itself is ridiculous. I am *thrilled* to be getting the fuck out of Yokel Land." Still, her lips twitched as she blew out the smoke. Later that afternoon, as a send-off gift, my father had a dozen white roses delivered, wrapped in shiny Yale-blue ribbon. They wilted, of course, in the August heat. My mother felt horrible for the flower boy, who was forced to drive all the way out from Charleston. She invited him to sit on the porch with us, and we spent the rest of Eloise's last afternoon at home drinking out of sweating glasses, talking about things that my sister would one day try hard to remember.

According to Eloise, Yale was the best place she had ever been. She called on Sundays, and we would pass the phone around and ask her questions. She didn't hate her roommates too much, she said. She loved biology class. Compared to the retard teachers at our high school, the profs up there *really fucking rocked*.

"Tiny," she said when it was my turn, "this place is amazing. You need a good kick in the ass so you'll study harder and end up somewhere like here."

"Is it pretty?" I asked.

"Yes," Eloise said. "I mean, in a cold kind of way."

"Dad said there's some secret club that you'll be asked to join if you're really cool. We were reading about it in a magazine."

"Oh, Skull and Bones. So lame. Completely antiquated."

"What?"

"Listen, go French kiss your pillow or something, OK? Be good. I have to go."

Life without Eloise was weird. The house was much quieter, and the phone barely rang anymore. My mother cleaned my sister's room as if she were dead, placing the pictures and the awards in careful rows. I went through her stuff when no one was home and found cigarettes and condoms, which I stole.

At first, my parents filled the void by paying more attention to me. My father tried to talk about books with me, and my mother took me to the mall to buy me clothes. I went along with it, but again and again I was forced to demonstrate how unlike Eloise I was. I didn't want to be a star; I wanted to be left alone in the school newspaper office. This was nothing they could brag about or even relate to. I made As in English, but Cs in everything else. And it was clear that I wouldn't be popular. Other than hanging out with my best friend, Charlotte, I spent most of my time with Denny Stillman, another editor at the paper.

Eventually my parents gave up, and instead of pinning any hope on me, they began to make up fantasies about Eloise's new life. "Up at Yale" became code for any reference to the magical place where my sister now resided, completely beyond our slow, daily drudgery.

"I bet Eloise doesn't have to worry about making breakfast up at Yale," my mother would say, stirring grits in the morning.

"Oh, no," my dad would answer. "Those Yale kids, they have their own chefs."

"No one ever has to take the garbage out up at Yale," Dad would say, loading up the truck for the dump.

"Of course not," my mother would reply. "Eloise never has to worry about garbage again. Why would you have to know how to clean if you've got a degree from Yale?"

When the phone rang on Sundays, we'd look at it almost with surprise. Eloise's calls remained cheerful through warm September, defiant through the red-brown fall. We each pictured Eloise's life up there differently, I think. My father dreamed of groundbreaking fieldwork, my mother of glamorous parties swarming with tux-clad Ivy League men. My own vision was pretty simple — just Eloise walking around with other smart Yale friends, sharing cigarettes. None of us really got close.

The day Eloise came home for the holidays, we were all up by seven. My mother baked a turkey and a pecan pie, cleaned the house, and made me help her trim the tree so it would be cozy when Eloise came in. "She's home!" my father yelled from the driveway. I thought my mother would tackle my sister when she yanked the door open, but instead she gasped a little, standing back and taking in Eloise's new form.

My sister looked about five years older. She'd cut her hair short, and what was left had darkened from lack of sun. Her skin, once tan, was now pale, which brought out her delicate features. She'd lost weight, and wore hoop earrings and a black blazer over jeans. Eloise was still pretty, of course, but she was old pretty, as if she had jumped to twenty-five even though we knew, or hoped, that under the makeup she was really eighteen.

"Well," my mother finally said, "don't you look sophisticated!"

"Thanks," Eloise replied, and I was relieved to hear that, at the very least, her voice was the same. We carried her things to her room, where my mother had set out flowers on the dresser and bottled water in her bathroom, just like she was in a hotel. Eloise didn't offer any information right up, so we started dinner in silence, until my father, who apparently had been able to control his curiosity in the car, finally lost his composure, slammed his drink down, and demanded that she tell us about life up at Yale.

My sister smiled. I was used to her expressions, usually tinged with haughtiness, and was surprised to see that she was genuinely beaming as if she were really, really happy.

"Oh, Dad," she said. "It's just awesome."

"Your classes? You said your professors are sound?"

"Oh, yeah. My classes are fantastic."

"And you have friends?"

She giggled a little. "Good friends, Dad. Good friends."

"Great, great. What's your favorite class?"

"Um, Am Civ, probably. American Civilizations."

"American Civilizations?" my mother asked, eager to be included. She winked. "I didn't know we Americans *were* civilized."

"That's a horrible joke, Mom," Eloise answered, suddenly serious. "American Civilizations means all aspects of American culture, as in, *minority* issues. Like *African* American, and *Latin* American." She said this slowly and loudly, as if we spoke English as a second language. "I don't think you should be belittling such courses, especially given the fact that this very house was most likely *built* by slave labor."

"I just meant me as an American," my mother said, flustered. "Me not being civilized. Don't get angry, dear. I wasn't thinking about minorities."

"Listen, we are very fair-minded toward minorities," my father said. "We're all Democrats here."

"I'm not trying to PC you out." My parents looked at Eloise blankly. "I just think you should be aware. You know. It's tough to be aware in South Carolina."

"What?" my father asked. "What's wrong with South Carolina?"

"Are you kidding? What's *not* wrong with South Carolina? The Rebel flag over the statehouse? A segregationist in the Senate?" My sister speared a piece of broccoli and munched on it loudly. "Actually," she said, swallowing, "this brings up something I want to tell you." My sister held her fork toward us, prongs out, as if it were a weapon. "I have a new boyfriend."

My parents looked at each other, smiling. "Well," my mother said, "that didn't take long!"

"A Yale guy?" Dad asked.

"Yes," she said. My mother beamed. "He's a graduate student, actually."

"Wow! Slow down! So he's a bit older," my father said.

"A bit. Yes."

"Fine. Just don't let yourself get stuck with an older guy before you've had, um, experience — you know, dating some other men."

I snorted. It was pretty funny, the idea of my father prescribing Eloise more sex.

"Well. I'll try not to pigeonhole myself, Dad. Anyway. He's from Madagascar."

Even in our very classic, bordering-on-cliché Southern household, the silence that followed was a little heavy.

"Is that in Africa?" I finally asked.

"How neat!" my mother said a little too loudly.

"Yes," my father said. "Your mother and I have lots of African American acquaintances.

We're just glad that you've found someone you like."

"That's right. It's fantastic, darling!" my mother said.

"Good," Eloise said. "I'm glad you feel that way."

"Absolutely."

"Listen, I'm exhausted. Thanks for dinner." Then she stood and, as if to reassure us that she hadn't changed too radically, went upstairs without offering to help clean up.

After I finished the dishes, I followed my sister to her room.

"So, what's his name?"

"Jacob."

"And he's going to be a professor or something?"

"Or something...maybe a diplomat. He studies public policy."

"How'd you meet him?"

"We met at the library."

"And, he's —"

"Black," she said. "Thirty-one years old, Malagasy, and black."

"*Thirty-one?*"

I stopped. Stating the obvious, that this man was disgustingly ancient to me, would not help me keep my limbs intact during the rest of her visit.

"Don't tell Mom and Dad that he's thirty-one," she said. "They wouldn't understand."

"They might. I mean, they understood about him being black."

"Tell them, you little shit, and I'll put Nair in the shampoo bottle, swear it."

"You know what?" I said. "I'm hanging out with a guy a lot. I like him, I think. Denny Stillman."

For once, my sister looked at me with interest. "Denny Stillman?"

"Yes. He's entering the science fair with me."

"Cute?"

"Yeah. Denny's white, though."

"I caught that, genius. Do you love him?"

"Um…" Mostly, Denny and I talked about how much we hated our math teacher. Love had never come up. "I'd make out with him. If he asked. So do you think you love Jacob?"

My sister picked at a loose fingernail and then

looked away. "Oh, Tiny," she said, "you have no idea."

By the next morning, my parents seemed to have decided between themselves that Eloise having a graduate-student boyfriend from Madagascar was definitely OK. Even though I heard them use the word "phase" more than once, they asked after him every time he called the house over the break and made overly friendly conversation with him whenever my sister was too slow to get to the phone first. My mother started bragging about her multicultural daughter at the grocery store and at church, and I knew soon everyone would know that Eloise had a black boyfriend, and that, even though she wasn't even there anymore, she'd still manage to be the coolest girl at my school.

The most disconcerting part of my sister's visit may have been the fact that she actually seemed to be in love. She spent long mornings staring moodily out the window, and when the phone rang, she jumped. "All right, baby," she'd say, right there in the middle of the kitchen so that everyone could hear her. "Love you too, sweetheart." Everything, be it food, clothes, or cleaning products, had to do with Jacob. "Jacob will *love* this skirt," she said when she opened a Christmas gift. "I can't wait to show Jacob this manicure set!"

"She'll get normal again, right?" I asked my parents.

"Please. This is *Eloise* we're talking about. This guy is just the beginning," my father said. "Wild oats. Let's just hope she doesn't break the poor guy's heart."

Eloise's second parting for school was not as much of a big deal. My mother made dinner that was a little more lavish than usual, but there were no flowers, and when my father took her to the airport, my mother, instead of adopting the full-on depression of the fall, simply busied herself with reorganizing everyone's sock drawers.

Meanwhile, things were progressing in an interesting way with Denny Stillman. I had always liked Denny, but since Eloise's visit, he'd grown fascinating to me. I liked how his glasses slipped down his nose when he was editing a piece and how his lips moved silently when he went over something that he'd written. I found myself trying to make him laugh. I knew that Eloise would think he was a nerd; his lips got caught in his braces, and he always hung out in the breezeway with the rest of the geeks. But this made him even better somehow, because no one else would take him away.

Then, in February, at my friend Annie's Valentine's Day party, Annie's mom left us alone "to mingle," meaning she was sick of chaperoning twenty fifteen-year-olds and needed a drink. Annie had invited Denny, and as soon as a sticky soda bottle was laid on the floor for a game of Seven Minutes in Heaven, I knew, with uncharacteristic calm, what would happen. Denny spun the bottle. It landed right on me.

Everyone was yelling and laughing. Denny stood up and pulled me into a closet filled with old suitcases. We stood there for a moment, breathing nervously, until finally he put his hands on my shoulders and kissed me. It wasn't really how I wanted it to be, because Denny Stillman didn't know what to do with his tongue.

Also, he'd been eating pepperoni, which was too bad. But still, I French kissed Denny Stillman back, my tongue mashing and sliding awkwardly against his, and when we were finished, even though I knew I wasn't really Denny's girlfriend, I wondered if my sister could possibly be as happy about Madagascar Jacob as I was coming out of that closet, pepperoni kiss on my face.

Then, in late April, I was summoned.

It was soccer season. A crisp but warm day when the field, which had been flat and dead throughout earlier months of practice, was beginning to edge slowly to green. The smell of it was driving us wild. It was a fierce game. I scored three goals, mainly for Denny Stillman's benefit. He'd gotten his braces off and wasn't hanging out at the paper nearly as much, but I thought the fact that I was one of the best forwards might get his attention back. It didn't. After the game I looked for him but was informed by his sheepish friend that he'd gotten a ride home at halftime with Annie, who, though fat, was gaining school-wide fame for her increasing generosity with blow jobs.

It was a long, sad carpool ride to my house, but my teammates politely ignored the tears that slid down my face. When I got home, my mother was waiting for me.

"Good game?" she asked, looking at the red-brown mud that caked my shins.

"We lost," I said, "but I did good."

"Well."

"Yeah?"

"I meant for you to say…" She sighed. "Anyway. Your sister called."

"Uh-huh."

"She wants you to call her."

I stopped at the bottom of the stairs. The notion of this, that my sister, Eloise — *Eloise* — actually wanted *me* to call *her,* stunned me more than Denny's betrayal.

"Am I in trouble?"

"No. She just wants to talk to you. Didn't say why." I could tell it was killing my mother that Eloise had something to tell me that she wouldn't share with her.

"I don't have her number."

"I'll get it for you," my mother said. "Why don't you go wash up?" I did, then took the number upstairs to my father's study, sat in his leather chair, and dialed.

The phone rang three times. Eloise picked up on the fourth.

"Hello?"

"Hi, Eloise."

"Oh. Hi, Tiny." I could hear someone talking in the background and a tiny sigh of exhaled smoke. "How are you?"

"Mom told me to call."

"Guess that means you're fine then."

"Oh. Sorry. Yeah. I'm good, except that I lost my soccer game today and I'm almost failing geometry, and I think that Denny doesn't like me anymore, so I thought I would have a boyfriend, but now I don't."

"Oh, well," she said. "Anyway, so, here's why I called: How would you like to come up and visit Yale?"

"OK. You mean, like, this summer?"

"No. I mean, like, in a couple of weeks."

"Why?"

"I don't know. I just thought you'd like to see

where I live. Come up for a weekend and get inspired by college and everything."

"OK," I said. "But why? I mean, can't I come next year or something? I don't have a plane ticket or anything."

"Dad will fucking *buy* you a ticket, Tiny." Another exhale. "Excuse the outburst. Your behavior is wearing on me."

"Sorry."

"Listen, just hand the phone over to Dad and I'll take care of it."

"All right. Well, awesome. I'd love to come. Thanks."

"You're welcome. You're going to love it here. I'll take you to some fun parties."

"OK." I paused, and we sat on opposite ends of the line, suspended in silence. "You wanna talk to Dad then?"

"Yeah. Put Dad on. And Tiny?"

"Yeah?"

"Bring a warm coat."

My mother packed my suitcase. It was a practical suitcase with wheels bought especially for the trip. She packed pressed khakis, two sweaters, jeans, and a fancy blue sundress and heels. My parents drove me to the airport in anxious silence, and when I got out of the car, they both kissed me.

"You will tell me all about it, won't you?" my mother asked. "You'll take pictures and call home?"

"It's just four days, Mom."

My father gave me fifty dollars and pulled her into the car. "Be good," he said, winking. "College visit. Chance of a lifetime!"

"For what?"

He looked at me, stumped. Obviously he had no idea why I was invited to Yale, either. We both knew there was no way in hell I'd ever cross its threshold as a student. "I don't know. Just look around. See if maybe Northern college is for you." He patted my head, then got in the car with my mother and drove away.

After my flight, I took a taxi to the campus. I had never been in a taxi before. I looked eagerly out the window, smoked a stolen cigarette, and watched the cold new world rush by. People wearing hats walked with their heads down against the wind. The streets and sidewalks were slick with frozen rain. The driver made his way to a mass of castlelike stone buildings, then deposited me and my suitcase on the wet, dirty curb.

I had never seen a place so gray. This is where Eloise lives, I thought. Even the people looked gray to me. I called to a boy about Eloise's age with a red cap and scarf.

"Excuse me?"

He halted, visibly annoyed.

"Yeah?"

"I'm looking for Eloise Walters," I said. "I'm her sister."

The boy shrugged. "Don't know her."

"Oh," I said, surprised. Maybe he didn't go to college here. "She lives in Saybrook."

"Over there," he said, pointing across the yard. "Just ask someone in that building."

I dragged my suitcase across the gravel path to the great stone building he had pointed out. Two girls were sitting out front, smoking.

"I'm looking for Eloise Walters," I said.

"Oh, she lives in my suite," one of them answered. She was deathly pale but pretty, with hair dyed blue-black and four earrings in one ear. She looked like a punk version of Snow White. "She's probably not there, though. She's usually out with Mr. Fucking International."

The other girl laughed. Snow White threw her cigarette onto the ground, then started coughing until she spat. I stepped back.

"I'm her sister. I'm up visiting from South Carolina."

"Oh. Hi." She looked me up and down. "You don't look that much like her."

"Can you show me where she lives, please?"

"Sure. Come on." She pressed a code into the keypad on the wall and flung the door open, and I followed her down a hospital-like corridor to a cramped, ancient-looking wood-paneled room filled with ashtrays, bottles of hair spray, shoes, and magazines.

Snow White banged on one of the closed doors off of the room. "Eloise?"

The door opened, and my sister emerged, wearing a frayed white sweater and lip gloss. I sighed with relief.

"Wow. Gracing us with your presence today," Snow White said. "Your sister's here."

"Tiny!" My sister smiled and hugged me. "Hi!"

"Hi," I said, trying to accept this sudden affection as normal behavior. I stepped into her room, which was covered in posters and housed two little desks and a set of bunk beds. It smelled like smoke and potato chips and perfume. "Cool room."

"It's abominable," she said. "We're like animals in here." I looked back for another glance at Snow White, but she was gone.

"It doesn't seem so bad."

"Doesn't matter. I'm usually at Jacob's. I won't be in here much longer anyway." She tossed her hair and looked at me. "How are you?"

"Good. I took a cab here."

"How urban of you." She laughed and hugged me again. I wiggled away. I hate girl hugs. "So," she said, "want to meet him?"

"Sure."

My sister checked her watch. "It's four thirty. We'll get a drink with him in a minute." She looked at my skirt-and-nice-button-down combo critically. "Is that what you want to wear out?"

"I...guess so."

"Here." She unzipped and opened my suit-case. "God, did Mom pack this? What the hell are you going to do with a sundress up here? It's twenty degrees outside."

"I don't know. Guess she thought I'd have to look nice."

"Jesus." She bit her lip and turned and threw open the door to her closet. She pulled out a green turtleneck sweater and a pair of beaded moccasins. "Take this. This'll look good on you. Just wear it with jeans."

"OK." I quickly shed my clothes and changed. My sister lit a cigarette.

"Want one?"

"OK." Eloise handed me a Camel and threw me a lighter. I lit it awkwardly, then followed her to the common room. She collapsed onto a chair and threw one booted leg over the arm-rest. I stared at her. She was still thin, like she had been at Christmas, but she looked more beautiful than ever. The weight loss had sharp-ened the perfect angles of her face.

"So, Tiny, what's going on? Still seeing Danny?"

"Denny. No. We were never really dating. He likes another girl now. Annie."

"I know that girl. She's a Camellia. I thought you were friends."

"I guess. She gives blow jobs."

My sister didn't answer. We smoked in silence. "So," she finally said, "are you excited to be here?"

"Yeah." I took a big drag and held it in, like my sister did. "But it's cold."

"I know. The weather drives me insane. There are some really smart people here, though. Famous people too. Like Marty, that girl who brought you up? Her mom's a big star on Broadway."

"Cool. Are y'all friends?"

"Not really. I don't know if you picked up on it, but she's kind of a bitch."

"How about your other roommates?"

"Not really." I looked at her, surprised. "I'm busy. I don't really have that many friends."

I put my cigarette into a soda can, puzzled. Where was her crowd? How could my sister not have a cult following by now?

"Anyway, I can't wait for you to meet Jacob,"

she said. "You're going to love him." She said this with authority, as if there were no possible room for doubt.

"Cool. Is he coming over?"

"Are you kidding?" she snorted, looking around. "He never comes here. No, we're going to his house."

"When?"

"Now. You ready?"

I said I was, and we put on our layers and headed out into the dark afternoon. It was still wet, but the wind had died, and the last bit of sun strained to show through the clouds. We walked quietly down a stone path, then another, passing girls and boys who smoked and hung on each other and strolled as if with great purpose, staring determinedly at the ground.

"Is that the Divinity School?" I asked, pointing to a tower I recognized.

"I don't know. How would I know that?"

"But it's famous, I think. Everyone sleds down the hill behind it during the winter when there's snow."

"Tiny, I don't even know what you're talking about. There's no hill there."

"There is." I knew that there was. Because I had been a victim of my parents' fantasies for months, I had memorized the Yale brochures. "Look." I grabbed her arm and pointed to the slope. The snowbank was slick with ice. Two girls lay in a heap, giggling hysterically, having just made it to the bottom using plastic trays as sleds. One of them sat up and waved, then laughed again, falling back in the dirty snow.

"Oh." My sister looked at them. "Well, no. The answer is, I don't sled."

Jacob did not live on campus. To get to his house, we left the boundaries of Yale and veered into a neighborhood of scruffy-looking old houses marked with peace flags and antigovernment stickers. Music funneled out of one of them loudly, and I looked up and saw a couple kissing heatedly on a porch above us. I stopped and stared. "Come on, narc," Eloise said, pulling on my sleeve. Finally we stopped at a dingy-looking red house with peeling paint surrounded by a decrepit gate.

"This is it," she said. She took a key out of her pocket and opened the door.

We stepped inside, greeted by warm, slightly musty air. It was a clean house, with a wooden floor and worn but nice furniture. A battered leather chair. A threadbare rug marked with an Asian print. A huge paper banner hung from the ceiling, painted messily with the words I LOVE LOIS. I wasn't surprised. Another guy, freaking out over my sister, I thought. Here we go.

"So what's that?" I asked, pointing to the sign. My sister opened her mouth to reply but then was grabbed and enveloped by the most beautiful man I'd ever seen.

Jacob was tall. That was the first thing I noticed. My sister looked small in his arms. He had broad, strong shoulders. He wore olive pants and a fitted sweater made out of something soft-looking. His eyes were the color of jade, his skin, cedarwood.

"Hey, baby," he said to my sister in a deep voice tinged by an accent I hadn't heard before. He twirled her around the floor, then kissed her as if they were lovers cruelly separated by time. I had never, and have not since, seen a couple quite so mesmerizing.

"You look so beautiful," he said. "*God,* look at you."

My sister blushed. "This is Tiny," she said, pointing at me.

"Sarah," Jacob said. "Hello." He disentangled himself from my sister, leaned down, and kissed me on the cheek. "Don't worry. I won't call you Tiny."

"Thanks," I said.

"Sit down," he said.

I took a seat on the deep cushions of his couch. I looked again at the banner. Had Jacob had sex with my sister on this couch? Maybe. The coffee table was littered with thick, impenetrable-looking books in languages I'd never seen before. I peered at them cautiously. Jacob was obviously pretty smart.

He sat down next to me and threw his arm casually over the back of the sofa. His fingers brushed my back. I stiffened and looked over at my sister, but she just stared at Jacob with a dazed smile on her face.

"So, Jacob," I said nervously, "you're from Africa?"

"Madagascar."

"Wow. I've never been there."

"Not many people have."

"What's it like?"

"Beautiful," he said, turning his whole body toward me. I had never been that close to a man before who was not related to me. I looked everywhere—the sofa cushion, his feet, the ugly painting over the fireplace—anything not to look at his face. "Quite varied, topographically. We have beaches with sand like corn starch." He pronounced it "stahtch," like an old movie star. "In other parts of the country, we have huge mountains of clay the color of blood."

"Weird," I said. "Do you have lions?"

Jacob laughed and squeezed my knee. "You are so funny."

"I'm not that funny."

"Lighten up, Tiny," my sister said.

"What? I just asked if there are lions in Jacob's part of Africa. I don't get what the big deal is."

"No big deal," Jacob said. "But we don't have lions. That's a different part of Africa. We have lemurs."

"Lemurs?"

"Like monkeys. Cross-pollinated with rats."

"Sounds gross," I said.

Jacob didn't answer. He sat back in the cushions and looked at me carefully. His hand was still on my leg. I felt my skin prickle.

"You're just as pretty as Lois," he said finally. "In a different way, of course. Back home, my brothers would die of craziness if they could see me with the two of you."

"Yeah, right," I said, but couldn't help blushing. It was like being paid a compliment by a superstar. "No way am I as pretty as my sister."

"Well, Lois is beautiful," he said, winking at her, "but there's nothing wrong with you being pretty too, is there?"

I shrugged. If there was an intelligent way to come up with a reply, I didn't know what it was.

"Tiny is totally pretty," Eloise said, lighting a cigarette. "She's just clueless, that's all."

"What do you mean," he said, "'clueless'?"

"As in, she doesn't have a clue. She doesn't get it."

"And how about you, Lois?" Jacob said, his face becoming suddenly grave. "Do you have all the answers?"

My sister lowered her eyes in an unfamiliar, bashful way I had never seen before. "I have some."

"Yes," he said, "I suppose you have some." They stared at each other quietly. I cleared my throat, wishing they would come back from whatever private, inaccessible territory they had just veered into. Something soft brushed my leg. I looked down, alarmed, only to see a skinny black dog leaning against my foot.

"Who's this?"

"That's Dog," Jacob said, patting the animal's side.

"You named your dog *Dog?*"

"He doesn't have a name. He's just a dog. He doesn't need one."

"But dogs do need names."

"Not in my country. They are just seen as pests there. We used to shoot stray dogs that came into the garden to eat our vegetables."

I blinked. God put dogs on this earth to keep us company and make us happy. I understood that different cultures had different norms. But shooting angels? This was hard to see.

"Y'all *shoot* dogs?" I said.

"Come on, Tiny," my sister said. "South Carolina is fucked up too. Dad shoots helpless deer for fun."

"We *eat* those deer."

"At any rate," Jacob said, "he's going away someday. He's not even mine. Lois gives him scraps, so I let him come around."

"Well," I said, watching Dog curl up at Jacob's feet, "he definitely thinks he's yours."

"Would you like something to drink?" Jacob asked. "Some tea? Wine?"

"Tea, I guess?" I said.

Jacob nodded. "Lois?" he said. "Would you?"

My sister hesitated, then went into the kitchen. I stared at Jacob, shocked.

"You've got my sister making tea?" I said finally. "She doesn't even know how to boil water."

"Your sister does whatever she sets her mind to," Jacob said. "She is a brilliant woman."

"I know that. Everyone at school back home —"

"Tiny." My sister stepped quickly into the room again. "Please don't talk about school, OK?"

"Fine," I said. I felt trapped. I couldn't talk about home, couldn't explain what my sister was really like, couldn't even defend basic animal rights. I hated Yale.

Eloise went back into the kitchen, then returned carrying a steaming pot of tea. She frowned at Jacob's hand, which was still on my knee. I jumped up.

"I can help."

"Tiny, no," she barked. She put the teapot on the table with a clatter and plunked down three cups.

"Now, Beautiful-Yet-Clueless-Sarah," Jacob said, sitting forward, "will you do the honors?"

I glanced up at my sister and rolled my eyes. She ignored me. "Sure," I said. I sat up and poured the tea for the three of us. Jacob took a sip, then coughed.

"This is so bitter! Jesus, Lois, did you put any honey in this at all?"

My sister reddened. "I did. I thought this was the way we did it last time."

"I think you made it too strong. It's horrible. Here." He handed her the pot. "Make some more."

"She doesn't have to," I said. "I don't really want tea anymore."

"Tiny, it's no big deal."

"Sarah, your sister can do it. Don't worry."

My voice got louder. "No. I don't want tea." They stared at me. "I want wine."

"Tiny—"

"Lois," Jacob interrupted, laughing, "if your sister wants wine, let's give her wine. Forget the tea." He got up, took the tray from her, and kissed the edge of her collarbone. My sister recoiled as if hit by an electric shock, then leaned gently back into the wall. I looked away.

"Sit," he said to her, then left the room. She obeyed, falling onto the sofa.

"What's going on?" I asked. "Since when do you make tea?"

"Shut up, Tiny."

"I just think it's weird, that's all."

Eloise's jaw moved in a way that told me she was grinding her teeth. "In Jacob's country, the women make and serve the tea."

"What, the men in Madagascar can't figure out how to put hot water into a pot?"

"It's complicated. Listen, I know it's weird,

but let's just imagine, for a *millisecond,* that you've left South Carolina more than once, OK, and that you know things might be radically different somewhere else."

"I've left South Carolina."

"You've been to Hawaii. And Georgia. But have you been to Africa? To a place where AIDS is everywhere, where mothers feed their entire family on a can of beans, where people keep their social structure the way it is, even if *we* don't get it, just so that they can concentrate on survival?"

"How do you know all this?" I asked. "When was the last time *you* were in Africa?"

"She hasn't been to Africa." Jacob reentered, carrying a bottle of wine and three glasses. "Lois, stop lecturing your sister."

"But she's—"

"You're being childish," he said curtly. It wasn't clear which of us he was talking to. We both fell silent. "Have some wine," he said, looking at each of us with an individual disapproving stare. If I hadn't known it before, I knew it then for sure. Jacob and I would not be friends.

We had Ethiopian for dinner. I wanted to eat at a Malagasy restaurant so I could see if it was true that only women serve the tea, but there was no restaurant of that description in the New Haven area. Jacob and Eloise sat across from me. He kept his arm securely around my sister until the food came. Every few minutes, they would look at each other, entranced, and kiss. Everyone around us was staring. I didn't blame them. It was hard not to stare at Jacob.

"Guys," I said, annoyed. "Come on."

Jacob kissed my sister again and smiled. "Aren't you in love, Sarah?"

"I used to like a guy, but he dumped me for a girl who gives—"

"He was a loser," my sister interrupted. Apparently the women in Madagascar could pour all the hot drinks they wanted, but discussing oral sex was out of the question.

"That's a shame," Jacob said gently, as if my Denny Stillman problem were the most important issue in the world. "This boy sounds stupid. Anyway, you will fall in love again."

"I doubt it."

"Well." He turned to my sister and kissed her. "That, also, is a shame."

The food arrived with beer. No one seemed to care that I was drinking. The more they made out, the more I drank in order to ignore them. Ethiopian wasn't like any food I'd had before. A huge disc of warm, flat bread arrived, surrounded by several bowls filled with strange-looking steaming substances.

"What do I do with this stuff?" I asked.

"Here." Jacob ripped off a piece of the bread with his hand, then dipped it in a thick paste of sauce and spices. "Open your mouth."

"That's all right."

"Just try."

"No, I'll order soup or something."

"What, are you scared of me?" Jacob asked tauntingly.

"Fine." I opened my mouth. Gently, Jacob pressed the bread to my lips while my sister watched. I drew back and chewed. It tasted foreign yet familiar, as if someone had added something weird to my mother's baked-bean recipe.

"Do you like it?" he asked, staring intently at my face.

"Sure," I said sullenly, not willing to give in.

"We come here all the time," my sister said, leaning into him. He smiled and kissed her on the cheek. After two beers, my sister excused herself. Jacob watched her, then turned to me and leaned in close.

"Well, Sarah," he said, "I am so very glad to meet you."

"Thanks." I was a little drunk but still on the defense. I licked my fingers.

"It's important to us that you are here. You know that, don't you?"

"Sure. I was surprised she invited me. But, whatever."

"Why?" Jacob asked. He put his hand on my arm. I looked into his green, seemingly concerned eyes and felt my resistance wavering a little. I could at least try to be nice. Maybe he was just having a hard time communicating with me, being from Africa and all.

"I mean, Eloise doesn't always want me around. I'm just the little sister. Do you have sisters?"

"I have three sisters and two brothers," he said, taking his hand away to sip his beer.

"Are they in America?"

"No. My entire family lives in Antanan-arivo."

"Where?"

"Tana. You can call it Tana."

"Do they visit?"

"They don't visit. My family is poor. They don't have visas, and besides, my family can't afford it."

I didn't believe this at all. Nothing about Jacob said poor. "But isn't Yale expensive?"

"It is if you're a college student, like Lois. I'm a graduate student. They pay me to go here. So I'm all right."

"For how long do they pay you?" I asked. "Forever?"

"No," he said. "Not forever."

Eloise finally came back. She had put on lipstick that was a little too dark. "What's going on?" she asked, and I saw that some of it was on her teeth.

"I'm talking to your sister."

"About what?"

"About things."

Eloise looked at me inquisitively. I shrugged.

"Jacob," she said, frowning at me, "I think we should tell her now."

"Tell me what?" I said.

"No," Jacob said. "Let her finish eating."

"I'm done eating."

"Come on, Jacob. I want my sister to know what's going on."

"Yeah," I said. "I'm old enough. You guys can tell me anything."

Jacob ignored me. "I think we should wait."

"Fine." Eloise sat down and sipped her beer. "Fuck it."

I didn't understand why my sister was so mad. Of all the lame things Jacob had said and done so far, this was certainly the least upsetting.

"Don't be obtuse, Lois," Jacob said.

"I'm not being obtuse. I'm drinking my beer."

Jacob looked at her face carefully. "You put on too much makeup in the bathroom."

"I just put on lipstick."

"I don't know why you do that. You don't need it. I think you look better without it."

"I like it." My sister touched her face carefully.

"But it doesn't look good."

"I think it looks nice," I said.

"It doesn't."

"Jacob—"

"You're not listening to me. The makeup makes you look common. You're gorgeous without it. You don't need to get painted up like some whore."

Eloise's face was bright red. "Jacob."

"Here." Jacob ripped his napkin out of his lap. The other tables were pointedly avoiding looking at us now. "Wipe it off."

"No, Jacob."

"Go ahead."

"You know what, Jacob?" Eloise stood up. I looked at my sister, and I was happy to see her eyes gleam with the familiar haughtiness that had been so sorely missing since we'd entered Jacob's house. "Fuck the fuck *off*."

She left the table and walked out the door. Someone in the restaurant whistled.

Jacob looked at me, eyebrows raised. He crossed his arms and leaned back, as if waiting for me to say something.

"You suck," I whispered.

He shook his head. I left it at that and ran outside after my sister.

"Eloise!" I called.

She had already booked it half a block. "Hurry the fuck up, Tiny," she said over her shoulder. In the dark I could see her furiously wiping her face with the back of her hand. I hurried to catch up with her.

"Light me a cigarette," she said. I fumbled through her purse as we walked, lit one up, and handed it to her, privately congratulating myself on how good I was getting at this new skill. She grabbed it and sucked at it as if it were a life force.

"He's such a fucking asshole sometimes."

"Yeah. He was pretty mean to you."

"I know," she said. She had stopped crying now. "I mean, what the fuck is *wrong* with me?"

"Nothing," I said. I was excited about this helpful new role I was assuming. I would fix everything.

"Whatever," she said. We took a sharp left. The campus buildings loomed ahead, black against the bruised-looking sky. We walked in silence while she smoked. It was starting to snow. I had been excited to see falling snow, but this was not the light, fluffy kind I had seen in pictures. It was heavy and unpleasant and clung determinedly to my nose and hair.

"You know why you're up here, right?"

I didn't answer. I didn't want her to know that I had no clue.

"I mean, you must have figured it out. The whole student-visa thing?"

"He said he had one. Because he's a graduate student or whatever."

"It ran out. He's done. We're getting married so he can stay here."

"What?"

"We're supposed to get married." She threw her cigarette onto the ground. It died with a hiss. "That's why I needed you here. I wanted you to be here for the wedding."

"Wedding?" I said. "Are you insane?"

"He's in love with me," she said. "And I'm crazy about him. Totally crazy."

"This whole *thing* is crazy," I said. I had to stop her. She couldn't marry Jacob. My sister was supposed to become the president or something, not some Malagasy asshole's wife.

"It didn't seem like that big of a deal," she said. "But now you're here, and he's being a dick, and I think that maybe I'm deranged."

"You know what your roommates call him, right? Mr. Fucking International?"

"I know what they call him, Tiny."

"Mom would kill you. You don't even have a dress."

My sister didn't say anything for a moment. I heard her hiccup slightly, and I thought she was crying. Alarmed, I put my hand on her arm, but then I realized that it was a laugh. It was a bitter, full belly laugh that made her body shake and her head tip back as she looked wildly up at the sky. Wet sleet fell steadily on her face as her laughter died. She wiped the frozen water off her cheeks, still smiling.

"They call this spring," she finally said. "Can you believe that?"

"Should we go back to your room?" I asked. I was tired. I wasn't used to wine and airplanes and secret weddings.

Eloise didn't answer. She was looking behind us. I turned and looked too. In the distance, about two blocks back, I could see Jacob's outline. As he came closer, I saw that he had left his coat at the restaurant. He was shivering.

"*Lois?*" he called.

"Don't talk to him," I said.

"*Lois?*" Jacob called again.

"Eloise," I said, "come on. Lois isn't your name."

She nodded, but I could see that she didn't hear me. Lois, sick with love, turned and walked back to the Malagasy man. I watched, hoping she wouldn't come out too broken. It's all you can do for people sometimes, no matter how much you love them. This was one of many things I was only beginning to understand.

LOVE BALLOON

THE TRUCK IS BIG and red and shiny. It's the biggest one in the church parking lot. It has a Dixie flag sticker on the window, a cap on the back that matches the paint, and a rack for a gun. It's June and hot and I've been kneeling and standing and thinking about boys and kissing, and on the way to our car my father looks over at it. There's this boy standing next to it — this beautiful, beautiful boy — and my father waves to him and says, "Nice truck."

"Thanks," the boy says. He opens the door and looks at me. He smiles, and the skies open. Then he gets in.

My father calls this boy the "farmer," and

he talks about him all the way home. He knows
the farmer's father. He tells us that the farmer
is nineteen and already running most of his
father's tomato farm. My father thinks he must
make, oh, forty thousand a year.

"He's rich!" I say.

"It's rude to talk about money," my mother
says. "And, Sarah, forty thousand is nothing."
She doesn't talk to country people and doesn't
like trucks, so I stay quiet, but when I get home
I spend the rest of the day thinking about the
farmer. His tan arms. His blond hair. His perfect pink lips. I think about how much I would
buy if I had forty thousand dollars. I think about
how it would taste to kiss his mouth.

Eleventh grade just ended, and I'm stuck out
here on the Island for the summer. I'd get a job,
but I have no car to get there. I'd get a car, but I
have no job to get me one. Lucky for me, Charlotte has a car, and because of the divorce, she's
been shipped to her dad's house down the road
for the whole summer. It's not that fun at her
house; it's dark and the whole place smells like

an old bag of Cheetos. But Charlotte already knows everybody out here, especially the boys.

These, of course, are not the preppy boys we go to school with; these are the dirt-in-the-cracks-of-the-hands kind of boys, farmhands and fishermen who, once school starts, we'll let drift away. They can't dance and we can't take them to town, not ever, Charlotte and I agree, *no*. But they're nice to us because they're country, and they're just glad to have any kind of girl along. They keep coolers for us full of beers and sodas and green boiled peanuts in Ziploc bags and tell us we're pretty as models. They're either blind or lying, but you know what? It's summer, and we don't care.

As soon as I get home, I call Charlotte and ask her about this farmer. Does she know him? Does J.T.? J.T. is the guy she's picked to go out with. He's tall and cute and has a fake ID.

She doesn't know him, she says, but I should go for it. I agree. Absolutely. Then we laugh, because I've never gone for anything. I've kissed snobby stupid Denny Stillman and that's it. It's almost senior year, and I'm the South's last virgin; while Bitsy and Annie and even nerdy, too-good-to-believe Prudence Smith have been making like rabbits all year, I've been alone in my virgin castle, if not untouchable, untouched.

Back in the day, I was dumb enough to believe Prudence and I were sisters, holding out together. We used to talk in the school newspaper office about how we were waiting for love. But then in study hall one day she giggled and told me she was dating Denny now and that they'd gone *all the way*.

"Is it love?" I asked her. She looked at me blankly, and I said, "Never mind. That's great!" But I could feel my heart breaking, seriously, it actually, physically broke, and the love for Denny that I'd been holding on to for two whole years, more than seven hundred days, it just leaked right out. Really. I could feel it, invisible and burning, running out from my ears and eyes and nose.

It's all right, though. It's OK. Because, guess what? It gets better. The heart, I mean. It's sort of like a big, bloody scrape that makes you cry in the morning and then starts closing up by noon. You know how I know? Because Charlotte just called back and told me the farmer's name is Lee, and I can't stop saying it. *Lee.* Lee! So goodbye, Denny. Dear Prudence, so long.

She says J.T. asked him to the bonfire tonight, and I almost don't think I can go, because if I see him I will explode, my guts will smear all over the cars, my entrails will drip down the oak trees along with the Spanish moss. But of course I'm going, duh, so I say so and hang up. And I should go downstairs and help my mother make dinner. I really should. She's having people over and keeps calling up, but I can't, sorry, Mom. All I can do right now is sit on this bed — it's a wonder, in fact, I'm even still clinging to this planet, far off as I am on my love balloon.

When I come down, there are people over for cocktails. I've put on a dress my mother asked for, the pattern of which resembles regurgitated rainbow sherbet. My parents always have people over for cocktails. They sit in pastels and drink frosty mint and bourbon out of silver cups. Tonight it's the Ravenels, not Bitsy's parents but their younger cousins by marriage, I think. While the rest of America has the

Joneses, Charleston has the Ravenels, and they come in all shapes and temperaments. The ones here tonight are dark from a recent sail to Bermuda. They are nice and speak of resorts and how the Bermudans use rum as bug spray, but talking to them drives me crazy right now. Is it time for the bonfire yet? I mean, come on, lady. I can barely see.

My mother's best friend, Georgia, is here too. Georgia is my favorite of the Camellias. She's loud and funny and stallion pretty, with big white teeth and black glossy hair that she wears in a braid down her back. She's an artist and not married, but I see her around town with different men all the time. If I weren't going to marry Lee and be his farm woman, I'd grow up to be just like her. Tonight she is wearing a printed skirt and riding boots and a tank top with no bra. When I see her, I take a look down and hate my dress and hate my mother too.

"Sarah, baby!" she says. "How are you, daughter?" She's my godmother, so I am sort of like her daughter, except she buys me beer sometimes, which my real mother would never do.

"Good," I say.

"You're not good," she says. "You're smitten."

"How do you know?"

"Takes one to know one," she says, and her face goes dark. I give her a what-are-you-talking-about-exactly look, my signature stare in which I raise one eyebrow and put my hands on my hips, and she laughs and shakes it off and grabs my shoulders. "So. Who is it, sister?"

"Nobody," I say, but I see Georgia whispering about me later; in the last pink minutes of the daylight, she pulls my mother by her hand to a dark room to tell her secrets.

Charlotte finally comes to get me after dinner. I'm in a hurry to leave, so I don't bother changing my dress. I kick off my shoes and put my feet up on the dash and smoke her cigarettes. We get to the site and they are all there like always, drinking beer and poking the fire, truck doors spread so the music can pour out. Only this time Lee is there too, just like Charlotte said he would be, but now that I see him in real life, I just want to vomit, because I've thrown my heart open for a boy who will never love me. I mean, how could he? Let's face it, I'm just a normal girl, while he is an out-of-this-world superboy from the far reaches of the universe. A boy like Lee, with his golden skin and eagle shoulders, deserves a silver goddess covered in sparkles. A mermaid, even, so they can swim away together. Hell, even the boys are staring at this farmer, and who can blame them? He's perfect to them too.

They clamor to talk to him. They jostle one another, gathering round.

"Lee," J.T. says, "did you see that flounder I gigged?"

Lee shrugs.

"It was a big one, Lee!" another says, then looks down, embarrassed.

"You should come with me," J.T. says. "You come whenever you want."

"All I have time to gig these days is tomatoes," Lee says. He looks up and smiles, and yup, there it is again, that pure-ray-of-sun smile, the kind God makes just to remind us of what he can do.

There is more talk of fish, and I go to the cooler to find something to make me less scared or at least think straight. I rummage for a while in the ice. Maybe I should put my head in there. When I stand up, Lee is beside me, staring down.

"So?" he says.

"Can I help you?" I ask, heart slamming.

"You're J.T.'s girlfriend's friend, right?"

"Right."

"He told me about you."

Oh, my God.

"What's your name?"

"Sarah Walters," I say.

"Oh, right. Your dad's the lawyer."

I nod, try to think of something to say to that, and then nod again.

"That's a nice dress."

"I know it's terrible. My mom made me wear it. It's stupid. I hate it. I'm sorry. I mean, not sorry, but, you know."

Lee raises his eyebrows.

"Excuse me," I say. "I should—"

Lee grabs my beer from me and, in one swift movement, pops the cap off against a tree.

"You should drink this," he says. He fastens his hand lightly to my wrist, and I swear, I think my arm will burn off. He is leading me somewhere, oh, God, I don't know where, I'd go anywhere he told me to, even hell, but no, it's just that he wants me to lean on a tailgate, facing the fire with everybody else.

"Sit with me," he says. "Here." He sits and I hop up next to him and he puts his arm around me and everyone stares — who wouldn't stare at this gorgeous person, hello. So that means that just for once, they are staring at me too. And I just know this is the best thing that will ever happen to me. How could it not be? So I promise you, Lord, I will keep this moment forever, front and center in the living box that is my mind.

The boys keep talking about boring things like fish and Garth Brooks. I look over at Charlotte, who smiles at me to say, *I know, Garth Brooks? Please, these boys are so country.*

And I beam back and say, *Oh, my God, who cares if they're the biggest rednecks in the world, they could eat live snakes and it wouldn't bother me, just look at this beautiful guy who's touching me, I am so in love.*

And she nods and laughs, and I laugh harder because Charlotte and I can talk that way to each other, no words needed at all.

In the next few minutes, another miracle happens, in the form of a coming storm. Summer storms sneak up quick on the Island; it can be the stillest night you've ever seen, and then the winds start out of nowhere, bringing black and purple clouds. The dogs lie under the beds. Thunder rocks your bones. We watch the wind bend the trees, and Lee says to me, "Party's over. Let me drive you home."

A miracle, I think, waving goodbye to Charlotte. I swear.

Inside, the truck is even more beautiful than I thought it would be. I've already imagined us together in it, kissing and driving into the sunset or maybe off to California, but I never thought about how it would smell like tobacco or about all the glowing buttons there would be to push. It has bench seats, so if he wants to, he can pull me over and wrap his arms around me, and I wish he would. Do it, Lee. Go ahead.

Lee reaches his long arm over the back of the seat. My body buzzes because I'm thinking he's about to touch me again, but then I hear ice clinking in a cooler, and instead he hands me a beer. He's not supposed to be drinking beer in his truck, and he definitely isn't allowed to have one while he's driving, but oh well, whatever. Beautiful people, they do what they want. We sip silently, heading down the dark oak-lined road.

"Turn left at Bohicket," I say.

He nods and turns on the radio, and I'm glad because I'm nervous I'll say something to make him go away. It's sort of all I can manage to do to just say *Left here. Make a right.* Then we are rolling up the dirt road to my house, bumping over the potholes. My father likes to say dirt roads lead to good things, and, well, here I am, looking for one. The Ravenels' car is gone, but Georgia's rusted old Bug is still in the driveway. She must have had too much to drink, I guess. Or else she doesn't want to drive home in the rain.

My thoughts are interrupted by Lee, who turns off the truck and goes in for one. Have you ever seen a pelican dive for a fish? That's pretty much what Lee does. It's so quick, I don't even have time to lick my lips. His tongue moves into my mouth, and I try to match what he is doing, but it's so fast that all I can do is think of butterfly wings. Then his hands are sliding over my lap and up my dress and oh, boy. Um. OK. I should tell him to stop, right? *No, that's the point, you doofus.* Isn't that crazy, I can hear Charlotte from all the way over here. But now things are moving further and moving and moving and something is building and building and bursting and oh, my God, oh, God, seriously, *What is going on?*

I pull away, still gripping his arms.

"What?" Lee asks. "Does that feel good?"

"Yes," I say, trying to breathe.

"You're cute," he says, going for my neck.

"Thank you very much," I say. I'm shaking now with something resembling fever. "I believe I need to go inside."

The farmer pulls back and looks at me, and I feel this wave of love pick me up and toss me far, far away, no land in sight.

"All right," he says. "I'm a gentleman." Then he kisses me again and puts his hands back up my dress. "You sure?" He is pressing against me, and I feel what Charlotte talks about when she mentions woodies, stiffies, boners, whatever. The rain is pounding on the top of the truck, a hundred boys stomping at once on my head, and how does this work, Charlotte, how, because I am so, so lost.

"You see," I say, "I have this thing."

He stops fooling with me but stays close. He's listening.

"What thing?"

"It's about love."

He grips my thigh. "Uh-huh?"

"Well, I want to have sex —"

"Yeah?"

"I mean, OK. Listen. When sex happens — to me — well, I want to be, you know, I want to be in love."

He pulls back a little bit and looks at me with his out-of-this-world eyes and says, "What, exactly, does 'in love' mean?"

And I laugh, I can't help it, because this lovely farmer of mine, doesn't he know he is asking the same question thousands — no, millions — of people, famous people, brilliant people, have been trying to answer since the beginning of time?

"I don't know," I say. "Let me think on it."

He nods and kisses me. "Get on out, then," he says. "Get."

I hop out in the rain and look at him through the open window.

"I hope I see you later," I say. "You know. Around."

He laughs. "You'll see me, Sarah Walters," he says, and I know that, whatever happens, that's definitely true, even if it's not in a real life way, but just within the boundaries of my dreams.

The next day Charlotte and I have to go downtown to a Camellia tea. I can't even tell you how much we hate Camellia teas. At teas they make us sit together on sofas and listen while we are told about good sorority choices and benne wafer recipes.

I try to fight it. "You and Georgia aren't going," I say to my mother. They are in the kitchen, making breakfast. Bacon sizzles and snaps in the pan. There are about a million empty wine bottles on the table. Dad's gone, and they look tired.

"We'll come to the next one," my mother says. "Besides, you're running wild out here. You need all the manners you can get."

Today's tea is at Bitsy's house, and I am bored, bored, bored. I sit on the soft sofa and stuff my mouth full of crab-salad sandwiches until Bitsy's mom gives me a look that says *Stop.*

"Tri Delt is always a good choice," Mrs. Mitchell is saying. "Kappa is fine in North Carolina and Virginia, but I can't speak for up North, of course."

Of course. That remark was aimed at me because Eloise went up North and I'm thinking of going that way for college too. Who knows, who cares? What I care about is Lee. He likes me. I know he does. Doesn't he? Does he love me? I love him, I think. I'm pretty sure I do. I know it's fast, but—

Then Charlotte digs her finger into my leg, and I'd say *Ow, stop,* but she's doing it in a something-is-wrong kind of way. I look around and see Bitsy staring out the window, mouth slightly open. She's got a teensy bit of crab salad on her face, which is pretty funny actually, but I turn to see what she's looking at, and oh, my God, it's Lee. He's standing on her lawn, wearing ripped khaki shorts and a white T-shirt. His hands are in his pockets and he's looking up at the house quizzically, as if imagining the possibilities inside.

"J.T.'s here too," Charlotte whispers. "Shit."

"Mom," Bitsy says loudly, "who's that? He's hot."

"I'm sure we don't know," Bitsy's mother sniffs. "Maybe he's with the gardeners."

The doorbell rings, and Charlotte and I die a little together. She grabs my hand as Mrs. Ravenel goes to the door. When she returns, she looks at us, Charlotte and me, as if we are made of the oiliest, smelliest, crabbiest pluff mud ever. We are bad, rotten oysters. We are wilting Camellias.

"Charlotte. Sarah. There is company for you."

"Yes, ma'am," we say. We get up, braving the Camellia stares—oh, these ladies can *stare*—and walk as quietly as we can outside to where the boys are. They are standing on the lawn; J.T. looks a little shifty, but Lee, oh, my Lord, could he be any more perfect? Can you take me away in your truck forever? I want to ask him. Can we get married and just run away?

I say: "Hi."

He says hello and looks up at the house again and then down and I realize that this big house is making him shy.

"We're going to the Island fish fry," J.T. says. "We were in at Luden's getting tackle and I saw your car, so I decided to stop, see if y'all wanted to go."

"We have beer," Lee says.

"You can leave your car," J.T. says.

I look at Charlotte.

We shouldn't go. They'll kill us, her face says.

Please, mine says. *It's worth getting killed. Just look at these boys.*

All right. For you only, hers says. *You owe me big.*

Forever, mine says.

"Let's go," Charlotte says to the boys. "Prison break."

We pile into J.T.'s station wagon, them in front, us in back, and J.T. peels off, right down South Battery. I don't look, but I can imagine the Camellia faces peeking out, frowning. We might get kicked out. I don't know if that's possible, it could happen, I suppose, but I don't care, because Lee reaches back and hands me a beer. Charlotte sings to the R.E.M. song on the radio and the wind is warm and is there any happier place than in a carful of kids driving toward the water with the windows open? Nope, Camellias. I think not.

The faster we go, the farther away they get, and Charlotte and I put our arms out the window and pretend the car has wings. We drink one beer and then another until I have to pee really, y'all, seriously, but that's OK because we're here.

Everyone comes to the fish fry: old money Islanders, farmers, new Kiawah people, blacks, whites — everybody. It's a church thing, but there's not much churchy about it; we're still drinking even though we've switched to paper cups to be sneaky. We are starving now, so we pay five dollars for all-you-can-eat fried flounder and hush puppies and okra and macaroni casserole. Onstage, the ladies from the black church sway and sing. They are singing like they are just positive God is right here, listening. And before yesterday, I'd wonder, How can you be so sure, ladies, how do you know? But I've got the best arm in the world draped around my shoulder, and I get it now. Seriously. So thank you, God. Thanks.

Which is right when Charlotte grabs me and whispers, "Hey. We've got to roll."

"Why?" I ask.

"Your mom's here," she says. "Her and Georgia. Look."

I turn to where her finger is pointing. I've been drinking a lot, so it's a bit hard for me to focus, but she's right. They are there together. My mother is talking to Georgia intently. She has the same patient look on her face as when she's trying to explain something to me I really don't understand, like *why* the regurgitated sherbet dress, or *why* the Camellia tea. Georgia looks like someone just died on her. Her mouth is turned down, her black eyes are open wide and are teary. Her face is the opposite of in love; it's the other side of it. It's terrifying enough to sober me up and say to everybody, "Let's go."

J.T. nods. He is smart and understands that parents mean danger. We put our heads down and walk to the car. It's almost dark now, so this time Charlotte rides up front and Lee rides in the back. He holds me right next to him and kisses me from time to time. I rub the spun-gold hairs on his knee and he sighs, happy. We are going to the beach, J.T. says, and that's fine with me, we're already in trouble from ditching the tea, so I'll go anywhere. I just wish I could get Georgia's face, cracked with misery, out of my head. I can't quite, though, even when we get to the beach, even when we split off to find cool spots in the dunes.

"You in love yet?" Lee asks after a while. He is looking at me with his grassy eyes, all of me, every inch, because we've found, what do you know, without clothes, we're even more perfect together than before.

"In love?" I repeat. I am not sure about *in* anymore. *In* means a place you dive into. *In* means, according to Georgia's haunted stare, a state that requires climbing out.

I look at this farmer hovering above me. He is so beautiful. Rising. Falling. He must have been there before, must have known if *in* was a place worth going.

"In love?" I say again, asking him to please, please tell.

He doesn't answer. He doesn't have one. He takes my words as a yes.

NORTH

W HEN THE GIRL goes North, the first thing she notices is the smell. The air at the college is sharp and woody. It's the cedar chips, she's told, used to line the flower beds. Later she will find this is to keep the frost from killing the roots.

Her mother packed for her. Southern mothers are fussy, and hers, in particular, is very concerned about clothes. When the girl arrives in her bare cinder-block dorm room, she opens her trunk to find it filled with impractical things like printed dresses and high heels. She shows the shoes to her roommate and makes fun of her mother. This makes the roommate giggle, and they begin to become friends.

The girl is excited to be in a new place. She wants to be liked and wants to make new friends, so she relies on her manners.

Hello, she says politely to a group of strangers. Where are y'all from?

This causes them to laugh hysterically. People gather around to listen to her accent, which makes the girl feel like she is on the wrong side of the glass at the zoo. After that, she curbs her "pleases" and yanks her "ma'ams." She keeps her vowels on a leash, venturing into conversations tentatively, as if she were a cub on a slippery log.

People dress differently in the North. The boys wear plaid flannel shirts and let their underwear peek from over the top of their pants; the girls never wear skirts, ever, only jeans and pullovers made of a substance called Synchilla. When the girl first hears this word, she thinks it might be a Spanish snack, but she is corrected by her roommate, who has become her guide. Both the girls and the boys wear baseball caps.

This is a private college, and most of these peo-ple are fairly wealthy, but the girl notices that, in terms of hats, the more worn out, the better. She hears one boy tell another that he put his new hat through the dishwasher on high in order to make it more frayed.

After the first month, she too begins to wear frayed things. The skirts her mother packed are pushed to the back of her closet. Her father's old down hunting jacket, packed at the last minute on a whim, moves up front. She saves her allow-ance and sends away for Synchilla. When it arrives, she tears open the box and puts it on; it's warm and softer than any cotton, and she buries her face in the material and understands.

There are new boys up North. The girl likes boys, so she takes note of their differences from the boys at home. Their laughs are squawky. Their manners are different. They do not sit up straight at the dining hall but hunch over their food; when they sit together, talking in the dorm lounges, they put their hands down the front of their pants to keep them warm. At first the girl is put off by their gruffness, but she comes to like these boys. They are faster than the boys at home. Sharper. More alive.

There is one boy in particular. Brett. He is a golden retriever of a boy, blond and friendly and always carrying a lacrosse stick. She sees him around campus, and then one night they begin talking at a party she attends with her roommate. He gives her a cup of purple punch and the walls churn and they kiss by the dappled light of a disco ball.

The first snow thrills her. She wakes up one morning, crammed in her bunk bed next to Brett, and the world is clean, and the dirt and mud and cedar chips—the smell of which she has come to hate—are magically erased. She dresses and pulls on her father's jacket and goes outside, pressing each foot into the white with a satisfying crunch. In the afternoon she and her new friends, the ones she now speaks with freely in clipped tones, make a fort and throw snowballs. Brett appears and tackles her. She is happy in the whiteness.

The cold. It is always there. People from the South tried to explain this to the girl before she left, but she doesn't understand, really, until she has to face it day after day after day. It is always waiting, gray and merciless, no matter how much she tries to wish it away. She fights it with sweaters and hats and her father's coat, but the slicing air finds its way through the zipper and every open pore in the wool of her scarf. Sometimes, it wins; there are days during the first winter when she looks at the ice-covered window and finds herself unable to leave her bed.

There is a structure to her Northern friends' behavior that she works to decipher. Her friends adore nicknames. They are always on the move. These were not children raised on porches; unless they are getting stoned, they never sit. Let's go, they like to say. Let's head out. There is much joy to be found in heading out, in going somewhere different than the moment before.

They speak of Miracles and Mango and the Deer and the Squire and Fish. The girl finds out that Fish is a band spelled with a "ph." A Miracle is a free ticket. Mango is a song. The Deer is an island. The Squire is a bar on Cape Cod. Eventually, she will go to these places. She will listen to this band. She will never understand what the lyrics to the Mango song mean.

Brett starts to float out more than in. The girl is learning that Northern college boys are atomic, kinetic beings. They roam from the dorm to the library, heads swiveling from side to side, always looking for the better thing. The girl does not understand at first that they are uncontainable; she is used to Southern boys, who just pick one girl for a while and stay. When she sees Brett with another girl at a party, it makes her cry. Her new friends explain that this is no big deal. You are only hooking up, they tell her. You should go hook up too.

The girl comes to understand hooking up. She goes to parties and lingers on the late side, drinking and bumping into heavy-lidded boys whose legs have become unsteady from beer. She learns to leave the boys' rooms early in the morning. She learns not to be alarmed when she wakes up not knowing where she is.

By the end of the first year, she does not talk to Brett anymore. She is no longer friends with her roommate. They separate, and the next year she moves into a house with other people. She watches the new girls arrive on campus in their skirts, and she and her now-old friends laugh at them.

Sometimes she calls her friends from back home. In the beginning, their voices are thick ropes thrown to her from the deck of a lifeboat. I miss y'all, she tells them, her accent creeping back. By the second and third years, she hardly talks to them at all. They see one another at home on vacation, but the need to phone one another has drifted and disappeared.

The girl feels less desire to go home on her vacations. She still travels there for holidays, of course, but she spends her summers with her new friends, working at the Squire and on the Deer. They rent cheap houses and sleep on floors and sofas and build fires outside at night and drink.

The girl becomes an excellent drinker. She learns that emptying her glass faster than the others garners shouts and cheering. She becomes able to flip a shiny quarter into a glass of beer from across the room. She learns to be able to work the day after, while vomiting on bathroom breaks. She learns how to discreetly inquire about her actions if she cannot remember what happened the night before.

By senior year, the girl has come not to mind the cold so much anymore. This is fortunate, because the last winter is long; it takes over most of the spring. Her friends travel often down to Boston and New York to interview for jobs. The girl does not know what kind of job she will get. She is excellently educated in twentieth-century feminist literature, but there are no jobs that care about that. She thinks about going home, but when she visits now, she feels like a tourist. She might travel for a while in Europe, she tells people. She has money saved from working at the Squire. Or she will go to New York, maybe. Everyone else is going there.

The last big snow is in May. No one can believe it is snowing in May. The friends in her house are disgruntled by the weather. She is tired of these friends. In New York they will not see one another much. She will return to her Southern friends; they will move to New York too.

Today her Northern friends are sitting indoors, complaining and smoking pot. She smokes pot with them, but it only makes the afternoon worse and she goes outside to get away. She still wears her father's hunting jacket when she goes out. It has proved to be her most prized possession.

She heads into the woods behind the library and walks on a trail. She has never been on this trail. It is beautiful. She should have found it sooner. Oh well, she thinks. She walks for a long time, mind buzzing, thinking about the nothingness that is coming next year. She loses the trail, but she is not worried; she walks in the woods often and knows how to follow her footprints home. She keeps walking and thinking and walking and thinking and it is getting darker and she realizes it is snowing. It has been snowing for quite a while. The flakes are big and heavy; she can't believe she hasn't noticed. She turns back, hurrying, before the snow covers what's left of the path she's made.

THERE'S ALWAYS SOMETHING

CHARLOTTE WAS my best friend. Back home, we used to tease our hair and wear cutoffs. We dipped. In the summers, we'd go down to one of our boyfriends' docks and float in the green river. But Charlotte and I knew we weren't meant to be with these boys. We knew we were destined to leave them. One afternoon we drifted away from them on the water, our thighs spread out over hot inner tubes.

"Someday we're going to be famous," Charlotte said.

"Famous," I said. I looked up at the sky. "Maybe. I don't know if I want to be famous."

"Well, everything will be what you want, I mean," she said. At the time, she had the bad habit of saying things that sounded like they were out of cheesy country songs. "You close your eyes and wish on the sun, and you'll get everything you wish for."

So I closed my eyes. She took my hand, and we tipped our heads back, our hair forming fans around us in the water as we pictured the prettier life we knew was ahead.

WHEN I WAS twenty-four, I moved with Charlotte to New York City. I was raised on the marsh, next to a silent river as warm and giving as blood, so at first, the city's sharpness made me crazy. I'd run to the closest pier on a full moon to watch the light on the water. I'd go to the fancy grocery store and splurge on fresh gardenias to put around our place. I'm worn in now, gray and cool like everyone else here, but back then I was still bright and clean. People would smile at me on the subway. They'd lean over and whisper, "Honey, where are you from?"

The apartment Charlotte found was your typical Lower East Side shoe box. Thin walls, mice, pipes that groaned and spat. Still I loved the neighborhood: tiny streets peppered by angry painters with peacock-colored fingertips and sturdy women from Sicily clutching armfuls of warm bread. It took us a while to shed our Southern ways, but after a few months we figured out that one's natural height should not be enhanced by one's bangs. Charlotte still had an accent, but four years at a Northern college had ironed mine out into a soft twang.

"We're going to a party tonight," Charlotte said to me one morning in January.

"We are?"

Charlotte was always in charge of everything. I just paid rent.

"Yes. Bitsy's."

"Oh." I burrowed under a quilt on the sofa. We didn't like Bitsy much. Ever since we were girls, one of Bitsy's favorite pastimes seemed to be making Charlotte and me feel inferior to her in looks and in social status. Still, as Camellias, we found ourselves bound to answering her calls and attending her social events. It was as if our mothers had programmed this allegiance into our psyches when we were born.

"She's still a twat, of course," Charlotte said. "But it's cool. She has a lot of man friends."

"Man friends." I don't always have the right response to things. Sometimes, when I can't think of something to say, I just repeat.

"Also, her friends kind of suck. Total snobs. So beware."

"Beware," I said.

WE WENT to the party.

It was one of the coldest nights of the year. Charlotte was apprenticing to be a fashion designer, so she played wardrobe manager while we drank straight from the Wild Turkey bottle. By the time we were done, I was slightly drunk and Charlotte was wearing velvet.

"That looks good," I told her. She shrugged, but it did. She had become a very velvet kind of girl.

Charlotte had dressed me in a small mini-skirt, so I was blue-lipped by the time we walked through Bitsy's door. The room was smoky but golden from the crooked halogen lamp. There were about twenty guys there, and only two women besides us. Bitsy looked like a model, with her blond hair, gazelle legs, and pointy shoes. She gave me a little wave and turned back to the group of men she was entertaining.

"Bitsy is always popular with the boys," I said.

"Bitsy's a whore," Charlotte whispered. "That's why we tolerate her."

I sat down on a worn couch next to a group of five. There was a visible shift as the boys looked at me: alligator bait in hungry waters.

"Hey, there." A short, jolly kid leaned forward.

"Hi."

"Nice skirt!" said the one next to him, handing me a drink. Tawny skin. Wire glasses. "Abbreviated elegance." The people on the sofa giggled. Embarrassed, I turned to the one next to me.

"What's *your* name?" I said. I was feeling a little flirty. Whiskey does that to me.

"Max." He didn't smile but angled his chin down and gave me a look that sent me spinning.

I took him home.

I say that brazenly. I say that as if I'm like Charlotte, a smart sex bandit who could get any man, anytime. This is not true. I'm a mouse with small breasts and strong, short legs. Without a bellyful of liquor, all I am is a woman who cracks stupid jokes to make up for being shy. Still, I asked him to come home with me, and when he did, I was happy. It was the simplest kind of happiness, the kind that comes so easily that, like water, you only think to question where it comes from when it's gone.

"So," he said the next morning, looking at me carefully.

"Hmmmm."

"You're a writer?"

"No. I'm a slave at a magazine. I get coffee. I shuffle through the slush pile."

"You want to be a writer."

"I think so. I just sold a little piece to the *Observer.*"

"Good," he said approvingly.

I'd already found out a couple of things about him the night before: he was six years older; he made money with money; and he lived way up on the Upper West Side near the American Museum of Natural History, a world away from me.

"I'll get you some water," he said. He got up, and I saw his back—a swimmer's back, marked with wide muscles working neatly under snowy skin.

"Are you hung over?" he asked, getting back in bed.

"God, yes. I just pray I have some cigarettes left. Jesus, I'm dying."

He frowned. "You smoke?"

"Oh," I said, kicking the ashtray under the bed with my dangling foot, "no, not really. I mean, only sometimes."

Max put his hand softly on my forehead.

The smoking was the first thing to go.

"WHO THE HELL was that?" asked Charlotte.

"That. Um, Max. From the party."

"Don't remember him." Charlotte had meant to meet someone too but had taken Ecstasy and blissed out on Bitsy's sofa instead.

"He seems nice." She made herself a Bloody Mary. "Nice manners."

I shrugged.

"Well," she said, "we'll see if he calls."

HE CALLED.

I PICKED the Rodeo Bar. Charlotte and I liked to go there sometimes and watch the fake cowboy bands, get drunk, sing our favorite love songs. We had learned that men found this endearing.

I was wearing my old boots and a shirt with sparkles on it. Charlotte raised her eyebrows. "Yee-haw. Back to the roots."

"Is it OK?"

She nodded. "Very cute. Very you."

I got there early and had a tequila shot. Max was ten minutes late. He blew in the door, his cheeks pink with cold. I'd forgotten how strik-ing he was. Max wasn't handsome in your clas-sic catalog way; his features were jagged and uneven, and there was a scar across his cheek that was never explained to me. Still, his height and curly black hair drew notice, as did the intense expression he wore. People were look-ing. When I saw his tweed coat, I found myself wishing very hard that I did not sparkle.

"I'm sorry," he said. "I ran six blocks. Didn't want to keep you waiting."

I smiled and looked down at my hands. They were shaking.

"I'D COME HOME with you," he said when we were leaving, "but you probably need your rest."

"That's right. I'm respectable."

"You're such a pretty girl." He kissed me lightly. I felt an electric shock, the kind I thought ended after sixteen. He walked me to the subway, where we separated. Him, uptown. Me, opposite.

"TELL ME EVERYTHING," Charlotte said from her mother's chair. At least it used to be her mother's, before the divorce. Charlotte had dragged it all the way up from South Carolina. On weekends she'd spend entire days there, covered in a blanket, studying different versions of *Vogue*.

I told her. I told her about the way he ran to meet me, his cheeks, the shock, the kiss.

"I love him," Charlotte said.

"Really?"

"Absolutely. I was worried about him knowing Bitsy, you know, since she's such a deranged slut and all. But it sounds like he has real first-class manners. He's perfect for you."

"I hope so."

Charlotte lit up. "Cigarette?"

"I quit," I said proudly.

"What?" Charlotte asked, sitting up with a frown.

BY THE END of the first month, I was spending the night with Max at least five times a week. I loved sleeping at his apartment. I loved the leather and suede furniture, the old lacrosse trophies, the bristled shaving brush on his sink. Everything was obviously better in this world of oak paneling and boarding schools that turned out men who wore bay rum instead of cologne. On the nights we didn't spend under his plaid comforter, he took me to dinners and private clubs with special keys.

Max devoured me. I had never experienced that before. Before him, sex was about a giggle and a bang, then a sprint to the bathroom to shower. This was different. The man peeled me open and turned me inside out.

"Every atom of you is precious," he whispered sometimes while we were drifting.

It was a time when I could only stop smiling to sleep.

AFTER TWO MONTHS, something important happened. Max asked me to meet his family.

"Wear the pink skirt," Charlotte told me, hovering in my room with a vodka tonic. "You know, the Nicole Miller one. It's perfect."

"I hate the pink skirt," I said, inexplicably annoyed. I chose a black dress instead. At lunch, I realized it was too skimpy, so I ran out to buy a cardigan sweater to wear over it. Before going to Max's parents' place, I brushed my teeth three times. I got to the address ten minutes early.

It was a small building in the West Eighties, but there was still a doorman, and an elevator with walls of carved wood and an Oriental rug and a bench to sit on just in case you got tired during the ride. I got in and waved back at the doorman as the doors closed. Because I had never seen a bench in an elevator, I sat on it. I looked at my reflection in the brass doors and practiced greeting Max's parents.

And how are you this evening?

Yes, I summer on the Carolina coast!

I was still talking to the door when it opened, which was when I found out this wasn't the regular kind of elevator but rather the kind that opens right into an apartment.

Max rushed over, clearly concerned. "Why are you sitting? Are you all right?"

"Yes, I just didn't know — wait, the *elevator* is the door to the house?"

"Of course. We have the whole floor."

"But then, how do you lock it?"

"That's what the doorman's for."

"But what if it breaks and you get stuck in here?"

He laughed. "I love you."

I dropped my fire exit concerns and loved him back.

The apartment looked like the inside of a pretty house you'd imagine in England, laced with antiques and wallpaper with heavy grapes on vines.

"We're so glad to meet you," said the mother. (Black dress, little diamond earrings.)

"And what does the pretty lady drink?" asked the father. (Wool jacket, old-timey pocket watch.)

"Bourbon and Coke," I said, and was led to a sofa covered in a buttery material the same color as the inside of a ripe peach.

The mother left to attend other guests, and the father sat beside me. I was formally trained in the South; I know the proper way to charm men, and I understood, from the way Max was watching me, that it was important to be charming at this party. I leaned in close and asked his father questions about his job, his golf club, his university. We laughed about his crush on girls with Southern accents. Finally Max came over and frowned at us. His father left, murmuring something, as soon as Max sat down.

"You're doing very well," Max told me. I was so happy that I kissed him, and he put his arm around me like I was a prize, the kind you win in the coin toss at the county fair.

BACK AT HOME, drinking with Charlotte, I was not nice about the family. I lied and told Charlotte I thought the father was gay, that the apartment was heinous, and that everyone there had splintered wood rammed up their asses.

She laughed but didn't say much. She was laughing less than usual. I looked at her drink, the third one in half an hour. "Really, they're sort of sucky. I don't know if I can handle it."

"You love him, don't you?" Charlotte said. "You can handle it."

THEN, NEXT SATURDAY in bed, Max fell away from me.

"What's wrong?" I asked.

"I don't know."

"Is it me?"

"I don't know. No."

"Can I help you? Is there something I can do?"

"Stop talking," he said, turning and facing the wall.

This went on for nearly a week. I couldn't sleep. I went over it again and again in my head. Had I done something wrong? Had something changed?

"Should we try a different way?" I asked on the sixth night.

Max looked at me blankly. "Maybe." He sat up and stared out the window. His face scared me.

"Max?" I said. "Come back? Please?"

But he just ignored me. It was as if I weren't there. Finally he looked at me and left the room for a moment. He came back with two of his own silk ties.

"Turn over," he said, grabbing my wrists.

I did it, of course. I would have done anything.

SOMETIMES, LOOKING BACK on things that have happened to me, I can pin down exact moments when certain situations began to unravel. *That's* when I should have said something about Charlotte's drinking. *That's* when I should have stopped talking to my friend's husband. But there was no hard beginning to where I went wrong with Max. All I know is that once I was in, I dove deep.

I started getting bruises. Charlotte didn't notice because I wasn't ever home, and what was visible I covered with makeup. In truth, I loved the bruises; they meant that he loved me as violently as I loved him. And I gave him bruises too. I was learning to bite and scratch. Our lovemaking was growing more and more violent, until it got to the point where I was surprised when

I didn't find blood somewhere in the course of making the bed.

Once, he smashed my nose against the headboard. I'd never seen anyone so scared for me. He cradled my head in his lap, rocking me back and forth and holding a bag of ice to my face.

"I'm so sorry," he said, his voice shaking. "I love you so much."

"I know," I said. "I won't tell anyone."

"You can," he said. "In fact, maybe you should. I don't think this is normal."

I looked at him thoughtfully, at the drops of my blood that were on his hands. I thought about my mother, what she says about men: that no matter what, there's always something. Fall in love, and you'll find it. He will steal, or drink, or dress up in your clothes, or die on you at dinner. That's love, she says. That's what you sign up for.

"Maybe you should get a softer headboard," I said, and to my delight, he laughed.

ONE NIGHT, I needed a break. I wanted to drink wine and talk to a girl.

"How long will you be gone?" Max asked.

"Just a couple of hours."

"I'll miss you."

"I know."

"I need you," he said, pulling me to him. "I want you to keep more things here."

"I keep lots of things here."

"I want more," he said, holding me.

I met Charlotte and Bitsy at Charlotte's favorite neighborhood spot, a dark, sticky bar with a juke full of Hank Williams. Lately, it had been transitioning into a gay hot spot. Lesbians slipped into the bathroom together in twos and threes. A woman smiled at me in passing.

"She's into you," Bitsy said, winking at me. "Gonna go for it?"

"She can't," Charlotte said. "She's in love."

"Who is it?" Bitsy asked.

I told her.

"Oh, wow, what a hottie."

I wasn't able to stop myself from smiling. Charlotte rolled her eyes.

"You know," Bitsy continued, "he went to college with my brother. Of course, he did have a lot of trouble there. I think he left for a year or something."

"Max is a hellion?" I was proud.

"No, well, a little, maybe. But I meant the nerves thing."

(Silence.)

"You know about the nerves thing, right?"

Charlotte looked at me.

"Of course," I said.

"Not that it's a problem anymore."

"No." I picked up Charlotte's lit cigarette. "It's not a problem anymore."

IT TOOK ME two weeks to ask about the nerves thing.

"What, did Bitsy tell you?" Max said, smirking. "She's such a gossipy cunt."

"Can you just tell me what she was talking about?" I asked. I was making him salmon, but I am pretty bad at cooking. When I checked it, it looked burned on the outside, raw in the middle.

"Well, at school, I had some trouble with stress," he said.

"Oh. Well. We all have trouble with stress. I'm stressed right now! Right?"

"Yes, you are," he said, staring intently at the wall.

"I just want to let you know I'm OK with all this."

There was no answer.

"And that I understand."

He laughed.

"Understand? Yes, cute little Southern Miss, I bet you fucking understand."

I must have looked as shattered as I felt, because he softened. He buried his face in my hair.

"I don't think you should talk about this, sweetie. You're getting in a little over your head."

I'm already in, I wanted to say. I was too scared, though, so instead I just served him the fish.

"So, SERIOUSLY, what the fuck is going on over there?" Charlotte asked me two days later. I was still in my pajamas at three o'clock.

"Nothing. I'm just tired." I put my head in my hands. I was crying.

"Jesus, you're a fucking faucet. Here, I'll make you lunch." In my time of crisis, Charlotte was turning motherly. It suited her. She looked awake and sober. She made me a BLT and a whiskey sour. "Tell Auntie Charlotte your troubles."

I didn't say anything.

"Look, Bitsy told me all about Max's mood thing. Don't get all crazy about it. It's not a big deal. He just needs pills."

I loved Charlotte so much right then. "You think so?" I asked. "But then what do you think I should do?"

"Honestly, babe?" Charlotte placed her hands on my knees. "Run."

BUT I KNEW Charlotte was wrong about Max and me. You have to work at a relationship. Things don't become perfect overnight. She thought I was a sucker — I could see it. But I was happy to be a sucker. Maybe to see where I was coming from, you've got to be a sucker too.

I got my hair cut, colored it blonder. I put on his favorite outfit. I ordered in roast chicken, put it on the table with flowers.

When Max came home, I could tell he was feeling bad. He shuffled in, threw his bag on a chair.

"Honey?" I called after him. "I can help. Talk to me. Please."

But he didn't answer, just went into his room and shut the door.

ASSUMING CHARLOTTE would be at work, I snuck out of the office and went home to pick up some things. She wasn't at work, though. She was drinking in her chair.

"What the hell are you doing here?" she asked.

I froze. We'd stopped talking. E-mails only.

"Why aren't you at the studio?" I said.

"I was there all night getting them ready for the Paris ship." She looked terrible. Her green eyes were bloodshot.

"Coke?"

"I'll be able to sleep soon. One of the models gave me some Valium." She peered at me. "What's up with your hair? You look like a fucking mannequin."

"Thanks."

She crossed her legs and lit a cigarette. "You want to go for a drink or something?"

"God, Charlotte. It's one o'clock."

"Whatever. I was just hoping it would knock me out. I haven't slept for three days. You around later, though?"

"Probably not. I mean, I have work."

"This weekend?"

"Oh, I would, but I'm going to the Vineyard with the Max Parents. They have this old beach house and—"

The look on Charlotte's face stopped me

from finishing. Without blinking, I changed tacks. "It's going to be just us and the Max Parents. Very boring, surely."

"*Surely?*" She smirked. "Please, woman. Spare me."

MAX AND I flew to the island in his friend's plane. His family knew people like that, people who had planes. Of course, after riding the private elevator, I'd stopped even questioning these things.

"Thanks for the ride," I heard myself say as I hopped onto the runway with my bag.

To me, Martha's Vineyard was a living postcard. Bright white houses, green grass, neon-blue sea. When we arrived at the property, I saw a sort of farm next to the ocean. There was a pretty garden and a tennis court, cracked from the sun and salt.

"Horses!" I said, pointing out the window.

"That's Winnie," Max said, smiling. He was being himself again. He hadn't touched me in two weeks, and when he rubbed my arm, it made me ecstatic.

Everything was fine. Better than fine. The house was incredible — wide-plank wood floors and expansive views of the ocean. While his parents were at the beach, Max and I made frantic love in my room and then showered together before dinner. We went to the porch and sipped cocktails of rum and fresh lime juice that Max's father had learned to make in Brazil. He'd just traveled there, he said, looking for business prospects. We went inside to dinner and had lobster and corn and vegetables from Max's mother's garden. Max's mother was having a war with the neighbor over the borders of their shrubbery. Max's father was going elk hunting in Jackson in the late fall. I realized that I was on the inside of something wonderful.

I should call Charlotte, I thought, and then didn't.

MY LAST NIGHT THERE, I drank. I felt like I was underwater; it turned out I had nothing to say about Brazil, or elk, or shrubbery disputes. Max's father liked drinking and didn't seem to mind refilling my glass six times at dinner. One glass got me talking, three made me funny, but by the fifth I was sleepy, darkly staring at my plate of overripe strawberries doused in cream. Finally, I pushed away my plate and asked to be excused, trying hard not to slur.

Max smiled coolly and patted my arm. "Don't you want to stay?"

"Be'er not," I said. I tried to stand, but my arm knocked over his brandy. The sweet brown liquid seeped into the tablecloth.

"Max, get your girl to bed," I heard Max's father whisper. Max took my arm and steered me to the stairs. The last thing I saw was the mother's eyebrows meeting darkly in a disapproving frown.

Max tucked me in. "I know you're young and haven't figured out liquor yet, Sarah, but I was disappointed by your behavior tonight," he said. "It was embarrassing."

I slid up. "Seriously?"

"Drunk women are so unattractive. It's really not the prettiest side of you."

"But I'm a normal human person. I mean, there are lots of parts of me that aren't pretty."

"That doesn't mean I want to see them," he said, shutting the door.

I WOKE UP at three a.m. in a panic, heart beating, sweating, thinking of everything that was wrong. I was going to lose him. I knew it. My head pounded, and I crept to the bathroom to look for aspirin. The floorboards sighed under my weight. I heard someone moan and turn over.

Max's toiletry bag was on the sink, a worn, well-oiled bag made of good leather. Even pissed, I couldn't help smiling a little; it was such a respectable bag, the kind you would want a proper boyfriend or husband to have.

I will marry Max, I thought. Everything will be fine. That is what I want. I'll be good and fix everything. Then we will be married.

I stood there in the cornflower-themed bathroom, trying to picture our Vineyard wedding, but it only made me sicker, so I stopped and rooted through his bag, grabbing the unused bottles of pills.

Zoloft, Paxil, Xanax. Thinking of Charlotte,

I popped a Xanax, grabbed six more to bring home to her, and went back to bed.

She'll like these, I thought, drifting off. At least Charlotte will be happy with me.

WHEN I GOT BACK, I found a note from Charlotte.

Bad trip. Detox. Went home to South Carolina. Back in two weeks.

It was more than two weeks. Charlotte's father sent rent but kept her in South Carolina for two months. And when Charlotte returned, it was only to pack. Her new AA sponsor had recommended that she live in a special house as far away from her former "situation" as possible.

"You need a new apartment or a new roommate," she told me quietly. "I'm out."

"But I'm not an alcoholic," I said, crying a little. "I can stop drinking so you can get better."

"Sorry, babe," she said. "Just seeing you makes me want to use."

"I look that bad?"

"You know what I mean."

"I can't believe I didn't see this coming."

Charlotte didn't reply, and we were quiet for a moment.

"Listen," she finally said, "one of these step things has to do with telling people you've hurt that you're sorry. So I am."

"For what? For being such a bitch?"

"Yes."

"OK." I went to her bed, folded a pair of socks, and put them in her bag. I was glad to see her. She smelled like apricot soap and cigarettes. "I forgive you."

"And also, I'm sorry for lying."

I blinked.

"I said your boyfriend was perfect for you," Charlotte said. "He's not."

MY BOYFRIEND, actually, was doing very well.

Since the Vineyard, he had been in a lively mood. He and his father had been getting along better than usual, which cheered him in a way that I seemed not to be able to. He helped me find a studio apartment on West 71st Street, three blocks from his. It was nothing like the old Lower East Side neighborhood Charlotte and I loved: everyone here was swathed in fur and in clean, pressed blazers; there wasn't an unbathed artist or Italian baker in sight. Still, it was affordable. Rent control.

"It's so boring here," I said. "There's nothing around but Starbucks and grocery stores where strawberries cost twelve dollars a pound."

"It's safe," he said, unbuttoning my shirt. "And the commute is easy for me." Then he stopped listening and made love to me. I ignored this transgression, because I liked being made love to, but the fact was that ever since the night I got drunk, he'd been listening to me very little. I kept talking and trying, but he was slipping off. Sex was our only connection, and sometimes, when we were in the thick of it, I would go to that place where one is present yet far off, and an image would drift through my mind of an old stone wall—the same one every time—covered in moss, impenetrable.

❧

As it turned out, the commute did not matter very much to him. After the first two weeks, I just went to his place, because it was four times the size of mine and didn't smell like the neighbor's fried onions. I'd bring cheese, wine, overpriced strawberries.

He came home one night, humming. "I brokered a killer today," he said, kissing me distractedly.

"That's great."

I was exhausted. My boss, finally noticing that I'd been a useless zombie for months, had demanded an onslaught of fact-checking that required my presence in the office by seven in the morning. I'd arrived at Max's thirteen hours later and set up camp on his cool, suede-covered couch. It was the sort of couch you sink into magically, every limb supported by fluffed goose down. It felt like a permanent hug, and I'd learned to snuggle with it when Max was occupied with being catatonic.

"Do you want to go out?" he asked. "I feel like it."

I shrugged. He came over and sat down. I hadn't showered for two days and was back to smoking, sneaking cigarettes out the bathroom window.

"You look horrible. Why don't you put on something different?"

"Listen, I don't really think I'm feeling up to it," I said.

"Come on. I made reservations and everything."

"But you didn't even ask me. I mean, I'm going through a hard time. Work sucks, and this whole thing with Charlotte...Can't I be the sad one for a minute?"

"Jesus," he said. He stood up and looked at me. "That was fucking uncalled-for." He threw his jacket onto a chair. "You know, I really don't need this right now."

"Excuse me?" I asked, sitting up to say something—anything—but he'd already gone to dress.

As soon as he left, I was sorry.

I'm so stupid, I thought. Why didn't I just take a shower? Go out? It wasn't that hard to go out.

Things would be better when he came home.

I'd make things better. I took a bath and blew out my hair. I cleaned the apartment. I put on a low-cut sweater and jeans.

Where had he gone? He hadn't told me. I started to pace. For the first time since we'd met, he hadn't kissed me goodbye.

Midnight came and went. I tried to sleep on the couch but couldn't. One, one thirty, two. At two thirty I heard the door open and then voices. Max and a woman I did not know.

"JUST TRY IT," he said impatiently when I started crying.

"Please make her go."

"You need this," he said. "We need this."

"I love you, I'll do anything for you, but I'm not that kind of woman. I'm a debutante, for God's sake."

He looked at me intensely. I've never had anyone look at me that closely. It felt like he was making love to every pore.

He got up and poured me a tumbler of whiskey. "Drink this."

"All right." I closed my eyes and did it. The liquor calmed me. He poured me another. I finished that too. He held me and then led me to the bedroom, where she was waiting.

I wiped my eyes and kissed her. She was taller than me and had long red hair. Her tongue tasted of sour beer. The noise Max made while he watched was familiar — one of happiness.

BEING UNFAITHFUL to yourself is not as hard as you'd think.

I will never compromise myself for someone else, I always thought. I'll kill myself first. But it's so easy. It's like wearing earplugs. It's as if you've put your head under the pillow during a thunderstorm, so that all you can hear is the faint sound of muffled rain.

Surprisingly, afterward I fell asleep for a while. At five I woke, got up from the tangle of limbs, and went to the bathroom. It was still dark. The tiles in Max's shower were fuzzy. I fell to the toilet, naked, and vomited, then crawled into the bedroom to find my clothes. I looked up and saw that Max was watching me. I knelt next to him. He stared at me emptily. After a while, he turned over, and I dressed, went downstairs, and walked home.

BACK AT THE APARTMENT, I rummaged through my things. I threw clothes and magazines to the floor until I found the address of where she was, scrawled on a piece of paper. EMERGENCIES ONLY, she had written in capital letters.

This counts, I decided. I put on my pink skirt and went to get my friend.

It took a while to find her, because halfway houses are supposed to be unmarked. Plus it was in the West Village, a place where the logic of the streets mirrors that of the heart. It was seven thirty in the morning when I knocked on the door. No one, including Charlotte, was happy to see me.

"You reek of booze," she said, pulling me outside.

"I know."

"What happened?"

"Nothing good." I started crying.

"You're in love," Charlotte said. "Of course it's not good."

"Well, I think it's over, anyway."

"Don't kid yourself," she said. "This won't be over for a while."

Charlotte lit up a cigarette and offered me one. I took it.

"Listen, I have a recovery meeting in thirty." She put her arm through mine. "You can come if you want."

"I'd love to," I said, "but I can't. If I don't go to work, I'll get fired."

"You'd love to?" Charlotte said, laughing at my tireless ability to lie to myself. I laughed too, and we finished our cigarettes and went underground to the subway. We rode in silence. She held my hand.

"I have to change trains here," she finally said when we got to 14th Street. We stood up, and Charlotte squeezed my hand and left. To keep from crying, I made up my own stupid country song, one about big leather chairs and scars and a beautiful back. It's a pretty good tune, but it's not quite finished. The ending, it turns out, is taking a long time.

GIRLS IN TRUCKS

A NNIE WAS CHOPPING CELERY, listening for Price's motorcycle coming up the drive. She'd started the meal two
hours before, after spending another hour at
the organic grocery store, filling her basket with
fresh sugar peas, smoked bacon, corn grits, butter beans, chickens that ranged free. The trip
cost her seventy-three dollars and forty cents,
she said.

"Not that I can afford seventy-three dollars
and forty cents," she told me. "But never mind.
Fuck it. Love is worth bad credit."

I've known Annie since dancing school.
We are a strange bunch, the girls from dancing

school. We have nothing in common, Annie
and I, yet we talk often on the phone, even now
that we live hundreds of miles from each other.
Annie still lives in Charleston, although the rest
of us wised up and left a long time ago. She is
sweet and plump and gives too much. As for
Price, he is a friend. Smart, lean, hard. Lost, but
always looking. According to social standards,
Annie was too good for Price, but I thought
it might be a fair match. As good as you could
hope for, for a while.

"Love is not always worth bad credit," I said,
looking out my window at my view of an air
shaft. I turned over, wincing at the pile of dishes
in my sink. My studio was the kind of New York
apartment in which you could see the kitchen
from the bed; Max joked about how handy it
was that you could have sex all day and never
leave the room for provisions.

"Save your money," I said.

"I'm fine," she said. "I have to go."

When Price finally rang the buzzer that night,
it was nine thirty. Annie opened the door, smil-

ing. She's a big girl with a pretty face. She has round apple cheeks and brown eyes that crinkle in the corners when she smiles. She is especially pretty in a skirt. She wasn't wearing a skirt that night. She was wearing jeans, the kind meant for younger girls, the kind that sit too low on the hips. She stood on her toes, so he kissed her. Her lips tasted like brown sugar. Price pulled away and walked past her, tossed his jacket and helmet on a chair. He perched hesitatingly on the edge of Annie's couch.

Annie always told me that she wanted to pick up Price's things and place them permanently in her closet. She wanted to wrap herself around Price's tall, thin body, feed him, let him have everything. This is how Annie loves all men, but she loved Price especially fiercely. It was a fact that scared them both. That night, she didn't touch him, though. She knew Price couldn't be touched at first. He was restless. The first night, she'd thrown herself on him the minute he walked in the door. He'd shoved her off. Not a hard shove, just an automatic thing, a horse shaking at new reins. She'd cried. But it was OK after. The second time, she got it.

It's hard, figuring out what to get, isn't it? Annie knew that, of course, from the men she'd known before. She'd learned early on that sexual favors—a breast feel here, a blow job there—will earn you male attention for a day or two, but she'd never found a candidate willing to take on her virginity. When she finally, at twenty-four, rid herself of this burden with her cooking-school instructor, she didn't inform him of the significance of the act. He probably guessed from the sharp gasps and the blood, but if so, he didn't say anything. He just banged her and left her. From him, she got that crying doesn't help. From the manager of the last restaurant where she worked, she got not to ask too many questions. You make a mistake, they snap, you learn. It's just simple kitchen-grade trickery.

"How was your day?" she asked Price. She turned on the stove, threw a stick of butter on the frying pan. We Camellias were always telling Annie to keep it light with men. Don't weigh them down, we said to her. Just be funny. Light.

"Pretty normal," Price answered. Price painted houses. He liked it all right. He liked the sweet, sharp smell of turpentine and the fact that he made thirty-five dollars an hour. He didn't like the fact that for the last ten hours, he'd seen nothing but Martha Stewart's Mourning Dove Gray.

"Well, *my* day was crazy!" Annie told him. "Our shipment of high-gluten flour didn't come in, of course, and everyone wanted fresh bread and popovers. You know how long those take. So I was, like, Jake, *you* make the stupid popovers, I've got, like, thirteen orders of *mussels* fired."

"Right."

"And then we got some VIP in. Whatever, I mean, Jake claimed he was a VIP, some producer of some cable show, but he was so demanding, wanted everything on the side, no nuts, no butter, blah blah. He even told us we couldn't cook with broth, just water."

Price did not want to hear about the rules of low-fat cooking. Even in jeans, Annie looked pretty nice there in the kitchen. She'd look even nicer lying down.

"Turn off the stove," he said.

Annie ignored him. She poured the butter on the chicken and put it in the oven to roast.

"I mean, *try* making something decent for someone who wants everything cooked in water. It's crazy. You just can't."

"Come on, turn it off."

"I can't do this right now, Price." Annie's voice cracked slightly. "I already put the chicken in the oven."

"Turn it *off*."

With a loud breath she hoped sounded defiant, Annie snapped off the stove-top burner where the butter beans were boiling. The blue flame died with reluctance.

"Go lie down."

Slowly, Annie shuffled to the bedroom. She lay down on the bed and shut her eyes. Through the wall, she could hear Price rattling through his bag, grabbing brushes and tins of color. After a few minutes, he came into the room and sat next to the bed where Annie was lying.

"Take off your shirt."

Annie sighed, sat up, and obeyed.

"Take off your bra."

"Do you like it?" Annie asked eagerly. "It was a little expensive. I thought you might like this purple color."

"Take it off."

Annie reached her arms behind her back and unhooked the clasp. Her breasts fell out of the soft lace fabric. She crossed her arms across her chest and looked down, concentrating on the nice pink flowered pattern of her bedspread.

"Now lie down."

"Price—"

"I said lie down."

"I *hate* this."

"Come on, baby."

Annie frowned. Before Price, no one had ever called her baby, except, sometimes, the rough-fingered manager who'd shriek from behind during breaks in the walk-in. *Baby. Baby.* She heard the word, thought of her cheek rhythmically pounding against the wet, frost-covered steel.

Annie lay back as Price pulled off her jeans. She closed her eyes tightly as he removed her underwear and worked them, lightly, over her feet. Annie kept her eyes closed. She tucked away into the back of her mind, the place she went when she got her teeth cleaned or found herself on a slow elevator. She thought of recipes, went slowly over the instructions for a bittersweet chocolate soufflé.

Price set up his easel, tapped the brush lightly on the side of the can, and then painted a straight blue line down the white stretch of canvas. He watched as her beautiful nipples emerged slowly. He turned to his canvas. Today he would try them as mountainous peaks. Yes, pink mountains, metaphors for Mother Earth and the female chakra and...fuck, he didn't know. Baby milk?

Egg whites butter flour semisweet high-grade choco-late, Annie chanted to herself. *Sift the flour. Sift.*

Here's the thing about Price: he's pretty good at painting houses. But when it comes to pictures, he's pure crap.

It's true. He sucks. He has no talent. His friends dutifully attend the shows that he throws for himself. We buy his paintings for twenty bucks a pop, and when he pays the bar rounds, we call him the Artist. But he has no eye for color, and he hasn't quite mastered the whole perspective thing yet. Houses look like boxes, cats come out as goats. Annie, in all the paintings in his latest series, resembles a soft, bright pile of string.

"Modern," Annie said generously.

"Cool!" Price's friends assured him.

"Pretentious garbage void of sense or talent," the reviewer at the local paper wrote. "This guy couldn't paint his way out of a wet paper bag."

Screw them, anyway, Price always says. Who the fuck are they? Still, when the painting was finished, it was nothing but a swirling mess of blue and pink. Sighing, he put down the brush. At least Annie was still naked. She was napping now, snoring lightly. Price shook her awake, and she smiled. He climbed on top of her, pulled his pants down to his knees, and entered.

They didn't have the best sex, Price and Annie. Not like Max and I. When Annie would describe it, I would listen with pity. Price was too hurried; Annie was too placid. She was a bit of a throwback, at least with Price. She seemed to think of sex as something to be survived rather than participated in. Price couldn't say this didn't bother him, but he did try, lasted a good fifteen minutes until she moaned loudly. He knew it wasn't real, and he knew that she knew, but he came anyway, pretending that they came together, so that after, when they were lying there looking at the ceiling, they could both substitute fantasy into memory for truth.

"I love you," Annie said.

"You're sweet," Price told her. He kissed her head, and they lay there for one, two, three, eight minutes, until Annie moved away to clean herself up and Price got up to look at his painting again. It still wasn't good. He sighed and walked into the living room, looking at Annie's crap. She had a ton of crap—books, photographs of friends, other signs of permanence. Price was not sure that he was into permanence. He lived in a month-to-month outside of town. It was bare and cold. He slept at Annie's about four nights a week.

He picked up a book from the coffee table and sat down with it. *Barron's Encyclopedia of Dog Breeds.* As he flipped through, he saw that Annie had filled it with lime Post-its, marking the dogs she liked best.

Burmese Mountain Dog. Cold weather, the
   green Post-it said. Boston.
Pembroke Welsh Corgi. Good for big city, if
   we move.
Yellow Labrador Retriever. If Price gets job in
   Savannah.

Price closed the book and stood.
"Hurry, babe," he called. "I'm starving."

Once, Price called me about Annie while I
was at work. He had never called me before, and
this was not a good time to start. I am an assistant's assistant at a magazine, which technically
means I am a receptionist. Personal phone calls
are not in the job description.

"Price," I whispered, "I really need to talk to
you later."

"It's just that she loves me so much," he said.
"It's freaky."

"Yeah." I looked at a picture of Max that
I'd tacked to my bulletin board. We'd had a
fight, and he hadn't called me for a week. I was

drinking myself to sleep, waking nightly in a panic in an empty bed.

"I mean, it's not like I've given her any *reason* to love me this much."

"No," I agreed. "You haven't."

My boss came around the corner, and I hung up. As I filled out the day's FedEx labels, I thought:

If only we needed reasons.

In the next room, Annie was dressing again, wrestling her bra back on, buttoning her top. When she looked in the mirror, she saw that she was glowing. Or, at least, she thought she was glowing. That's what this was, right? Afterglow? Maybe she was just too warm.

"Oh, no," she said when she entered the kitchen. "I forgot the oven. The chicken's ruined."

"Let's go out."

"It's OK, I can whip something up."

"I can't stand to watch you do it all again. I'm sorry, Annie. I need to get out of here. Let's go out, then."

Together, they walked to Annie's car. Annie handed Price the keys. She was scared of his motorcycle, and her mother taught her always to give the car keys to a man at night. Annie suggested a grill downtown, ten minutes away. "I think you'll like this place," Annie said. "They're open late, and they have *great* eggplant."

"I sort of hate eggplant."

"You told me you liked eggplant."

"I changed my mind."

"Well, they have great chicken too. Organic and whatever."

"All right." Price nodded, irritated. He drummed his hands on the steering wheel.

"What's wrong?"

"Nothing."

"Really?"

"Yes."

"Have you thought any more about going up to Bitsy's house in Vermont this summer?"

"No."

"She says there's a lake and a dock and everything," Annie said. "I think we would love it."

Price stared at the road. "Listen, you know I can't commit to a whole week. I just got a call about a job in North Carolina, some mansion in Charlotte. I might be gone for six months any day now."

"Oh." Annie wanted to scream. She wanted to scratch Price's face. Instead she forced herself to hum and look at the passing houses.

"You could come visit me, maybe," Price said.

"You need to watch for this turn here."

"Do you think you would?"

"Would what?"

"Come out and visit?"

Annie finally looked over from the window. She stared hard at the man beside her.

"Yes, of course I would come to you. Anytime. Anywhere."

Price blinked.

"Well, let's not plan anything yet," he said. "I mean, nothing's set in stone."

Annie put her hands between her knees and pressed them together, digging her knuckles into the flesh. They were at a light, stopped beside a black truck marked on the side with a glistening stripe of silver. There were three girls in the truck, lined up in the cab. They were blond and young, younger than Annie. Eighteen. Maybe twenty. There was music pouring out of the window, and the girls rocked to it, their glittery shoulders swaying from side to side, their blond hair swinging. Annie wanted to be in that truck. She wanted to be with those girls, to be beautiful, singing. Those girls, they were moving on to somewhere. They weren't stuck in a too-old Jetta, waiting for something, anything to happen. They weren't wasting their lives on a man who couldn't even commit to liking eggplant.

"Where are you going?" Annie asked the girls, putting her head against the cool window.

"Me? Come on, Annie, I don't know. We've been over this. My life just isn't pinned down right now. You *know* I don't know."

"Not *you,* asshole."

Price looked over, surprised.

"Sorry," she said. "I mean, I didn't mean to say that. I wasn't talking to you. I'm sorry. I meant that truck."

"Those girls?" Price looked over at them. One of them smiled and waved. "Who knows? Hell, probably."

The light turned green. Still singing, the girls glided away.

Are you growing impatient? Wondering why I am telling this story? Or maybe you've got it nailed. It's a Camellia anecdote, right? It's about the Camellia who played by the rules and made it work. There's Charlotte, the wild druggie one; Bitsy, the sophisticated, snobby one; and Annie, the good one who stayed at home. This is about the good girl getting what she deserves. And she does deserve Price if she wants him, or someone better. Maybe Hugh Grant comes for a Southern vacation, happens upon adorable Annie covered in flour in the restaurant, and whisks her away to a castle. That's what should have happened to Annie, because, sometimes, what we all need is for the plain, good-hearted person to *win*.

Price and Annie drove in silence down an older street running north to south where everyone drives too fast. He turned on the radio and pushed in a tape, but it was Annie music—whiny, lovelorn—and he changed his mind and ejected it again. When he looked up, there was something moving in front of him. Brown, with green eyes. He blinked, trying to register which choice to make, but it was too late, and sickening sounds followed: a thump, a fall, the empty double-thud tires make when they roll over a body.

"Oh, my God."

"What?" Annie said. She'd missed it. "Did you blow a tire?"

"Shit."

"If you hurt the car, it's really OK."

"No. Shit. Shit. I hit a dog, I think."

"You hit a *dog?*" Annie shrieked. "You need to stop."

"I know. I *know*. I'm *going* to fucking stop." Price pulled the car to the side of the street. He put his hands over his face. Cars continued to rush past. *"Shit."*

"We need to get out."

"I don't know if I can do this."

"Price."

"Let's just keep driving."

"Jesus, Price, it might still be alive."

Price stared at his hands on the steering wheel, not moving.

"God." Annie pushed the car door open and ran to the middle of the street. Cars honked and swerved to avoid her.

"Fucking cow!" someone yelled from a Camaro. Annie didn't flinch. She leaned over the body. It was a big dog, with no collar. Annie is not afraid of dead things. At cooking school, she was required to learn to butcher living animals. She once spent four weeks at an organic-feed farm plucking the feathers off chickens, gutting pigs, pulling the kidneys out of rabbits and quail. She bent down and touched the dog. It was dead. Its tongue lolled out of its mouth; its bowels were moving in final defiance. She looked at its face. A mutt, pretty. It had a brown coat and a white star on its forehead. Annie sighed and rolled the corpse to the side of the road, out of the way of the rushing cars.

"Come over here," Annie called out to Price. "It's OK, Price. It died instantly."

"It's not OK! I fucking killed a dog!"

"Price, I just said it didn't feel any pain. Come on. I need you to help me move it."

Slowly, Price got out of the car. He walked

over to Annie and the dog. Annie saw that he was shaking.

"Just pick it up. Here, take the back end of it, OK?"

Together, they hoisted up the dead, warm dog and walked awkwardly back to Annie's sedan. "The trunk. It's locked," she said. "You have the keys."

Price dropped the back of the dog to reach into his front pocket; the animal fell, smacking the ground. Annie thought of the sound her bare hand made when she slapped and tenderized raw meat.

"Price."

"I'm sorry. *Christ.*"

"It's OK, sweetie."

Price opened the trunk, and they gently placed the dog in the back of the car. They stared at it, considering things.

"I can't drive anymore tonight, I think."

"OK." Annie took the keys. She wiped her forehead thoughtfully with the back of her hand. "Well, should we get dinner?"

"With this dog in the trunk? God, Annie!"

"Well, it's not like it's going anywhere."

"No, let's—I think we need to get rid of this thing. Let's call the owners."

"No collar," Annie said.

"Jesus, this is so fucked up!"

Annie looked at Price and was surprised by what she felt. She said nothing and got into the car. Price followed, silently.

"We'll bury it in my yard," Annie said. Price tried to think of something to say but couldn't, so he turned the radio on.

"Annie, I don't think I can—"

"Forget it," Annie said, putting her foot onto the accelerator. "Just help me get the dog next to the hole and go inside. I'll bury it myself."

Burying an animal is not easy. In the marshy area where Annie lives, it's important to bury deep; things have a way of working their way to the surface in the spongy ground during the rainy season and floods. She knew she'd have to go at least four feet in. It was a warm night. Annie put the blade of her shovel into the ground with fury, heaved all of her weight on it.

She was furious that the dog was dead, furious that she was laying it to rest alone. The dog lay facing her, tongue out, eyes rolled up.

"What the fuck is wrong with me?" she asked the corpse. It didn't have any answers, so she continued to dig, mud flying, the soil changing from dirt to sand to hard red clay. It took an hour before the hole was deep enough. She climbed out and looked again at the dog. Shit ran from its backside, and its paws stuck out awkwardly from its rigid legs. Annie is not religious, particularly, but she decided a prayer for the dog was appropriate. She wished it freedom, sunny days, wide green fields, whatever else it could ever wish for. She rolled the dog into the hole, and it landed with a thud. Annie covered the dog with mud and dirt, stomped the soil down, placed a potted fern on top, and then went back inside.

Price smoked in the living room, waiting for Annie to come back. He knew he'd failed. It was now one twenty in the morning, and he was tired, but still he knew that if he went to sleep, he'd be even more fucked than he already was. When Annie came in, she was wet with sweat. Her cheeks were flushed, her hands, arms, and legs covered with dirt. Price looked at her, his pretty peasant girl.

"Well, that sucked," she said.

"Babe, I'm sorry."

"It's OK. Whatever." She stepped into the other room and came out in a clean T-shirt and shorts. She ran the water, putting her hands under and soaping up. "God, I'm starving. I'm going to cook dinner again."

"OK." Price hovered in the kitchen while Annie boiled pasta, tossed it with garlic, fresh tomatoes, oil, and buffalo mozzarella. He watched as she began the salad. She picked up a washed carrot and chopped it, carefully, into little slivers. She tossed these carrots with lettuce and balsamic vinegar from Israel and virgin oil from Greece. She mixed in caramelized walnuts and organic cranberries, hand-dried. The carrots were tiny spears of color, beautiful in a bowl of sharp green. It occurred to Annie that Price would never, ever notice this color scheme she had chosen for him. It occurred to her that he would eat it when he wanted it and think, simply, *Good.*

"I don't want to see you anymore," Annie said.

"Annie."

Her cheeks flushed. "I mean it, Price. I'm sorry to say it, but you're a dead end."

Price was quiet. He played with a tomato, rolling it with his palm across the wooden cutting board.

"Let's just talk about this."

"Let's not."

"I just want you to know that..."

"What?" Annie asked. "What?"

"I don't even know."

Annie grabbed the tomato and diced it fiercely into tiny red bits.

Price put his hands in his pockets. "It's been a long fucking night."

"It has."

"You really want me to go?"

"Tomorrow."

Price was silent another moment. "I'm really not hungry."

"I know."

"Annie."

"Stop saying my name. I'm so *sick* of it."

"Baby, can I just do one last one?"

Annie gripped the handle of the knife.

"Just one more painting?"

She could kill him. She could slice his throat. At least something would happen, then. At least something would be different.

"Come on, baby. Please?"

Annie dropped the knife and headed to the bedroom, leaving the salad behind.

"Annie," Price said, bringing in his paint.

Annie didn't answer.

"Thanks for doing this, baby," he said.

"Just do it," she said, undressing.

"Tell me what you want," he said after a while.

"What I want?" Annie laughed for a long time, her thick body heaving with it. "Jesus. I want a nice man who is brave enough to pick up a dead dog."

"No, I mean—well. Tell me what you want me to paint."

"God, you *freak*. Why the fuck does it matter?"

"Just tell me what you want to see," Price said. "Come on, Annie. Please."

Annie looked at the ceiling. Hot tears pooled on the cloth beside either cheek.

"A house."

Nodding, Price dipped his brush in paint and brought it over to her. Annie gasped when she felt the cold paint on her naked white skin.

"What are you doing?"

"Go on."

"OK." Annie wiped her face. "A dog." She laughed bitterly.

The wet brush moved on its canvas, slowly down Annie's soft stomach.

"Flowers. Kids. People." Price drew his paintbrush quickly, lightly, over Annie's skin. "Sky. Rainbows. Trees. Light."

He worked fast, then faster, over her stomach and legs and then between.

"I don't know. I . . . don't know."

Annie arched her back, putting her arms up. She cried out as the Artist finally painted out a life that she recognized. Big. Bright. The next day she kicked him out. As soon as she did, of course, life opened up for her. A man did happen upon her in the kitchen—not Hugh Grant, but a nice real estate man who exclaims over her cooking and thinks she is a gift. But that last night, there was no perspective. Only long-wrestled, hard-reached beauty.

Blue breast sky. Red pubic birds. Billowing thigh clouds of dusky pink.

YOU ARE NOT ME

Y OU ARE NOT ME, but if you were, you'd wake up every morning at three a.m., sweating. Your stomach would be tied up in knots, and you'd wonder what it is that you're panicking about. You'd look so terrible your friend would slip you some of her prescription sleeping pills. You'd try not to take them, but about once a week you'd give in. You'd take two with a little glass of vodka, and then sleep for fifteen hours straight.

Here's why.

It is three weeks ago. I am sitting at a table with Bitsy and her husband, John, in one of those fusion restaurants, the kind where they serve fried chicken with wasabi in the batter and sushi with barbecue sauce. I am a struggling journalist and would never waste money on a place like this, but they are treating. Bitsy has, as my mother would say, done well for herself in the marriage department.

Our dinner comes. Mine involves a huge tower of fried rice noodles, artfully sculpted to resemble a tall white pagoda. I make a stupid comment about how its generous size resembles one of my former boyfriend's most distinctive features. That's when John looks at me strangely. He says, "Speaking of which."

"Speaking of which, what?" I say.

Bitsy and John glance back and forth in a smugly worried manner they tend to adopt around me. "I don't know if we should tell her," Bitsy says.

"Tell me what?" Silence. *"What?"*

"It's about Max," Bitsy says. These particular friends are not the loyal sort, so Max still sees Bitsy and John all the time. It's been more than a year and a half, and I still am not over him. Hearing his name makes me see green and red spots.

"What about Max?" I say. I try to be casual, but the question comes out loud and squeaky. Just then, the waitress arrives. Bitsy wants to send something back; it has too much pork, too little sauce. I sit there in silent torture while the server considers this. Another waiter comes over. Then the management. I watch in mock concern as if all I care about is the pork problem, but really all I want to do is strangle Bitsy.

Finally, the details are worked out. Bitsy looks over.

"What were we talking about?"

"Max," I say carefully.

"Oh, sorry," she says. "Max has a new girlfriend."

OK. OK. I knew this would happen. I knew that someday—

"A Chinese girl," John says.

"A Chinese girl," I repeat, stupidly. "From China?"

"From China," he says.

John and Bitsy instinctively lean in together. They stare at me over their cocktails, waiting for me to explode.

"China? Really? As in China China?"

John bursts out laughing. Bitsy cocks her pretty blond head and looks at me.

I'd expected hatred. I'd expected to feel nauseated from the sheer spite. Now, what I feel is —

China?

Of course I've pictured Max with other girls before. I painted the picture the moment we broke up. In my head, the girls who get to touch him now are WASPy, rose-cheeked girls named Persephone and Gwynn who can carry on witty conversation while whipping up a seventeen-layered cake. A Chinese girl is different. A Chinese girl is like an alien, all the way from outer space.

"She's small," Bitsy says. "She has an accent."

"Is she…" I stop. I don't know what to ask. I picture a kimono. No. That's Japan. China has dragons. And the Red Army. And child geniuses. I bet that she's a genius. A Chinese genius girlfriend.

"She's really cute!" (Bitsy.)

"She owns a shoe store." (John.)

"It's not a big deal."

"Just the submissive concubine thing."

"Yellow fever."

"Asian fetish."

"Karate chop!"

Bitsy and John are racist assholes. I nod and encourage them to say worse things, and they do, about good laundry and lotus feet and how many Chinese girls does it take to give a hand job with those tiny fingers? They even make bigger asses of themselves by pulling their blue eyes into slits with their fingers and yelling, "No mo yankee my wankee! Haw haw!" Their faces turn beet red, and they spurt liquor through their noses. It's disgusting. It makes me feel better.

"Not that you care, right?" Bitsy says, finally sobering for a minute. "I mean, you're so over him, right?"

"So over him," I say, taking a sip of one of their drinks. My hand is shaking, and I miss my mouth. Sticky pink liquid dribbles into my cleavage. Bitsy and John kindly ignore this slip. They are, it seems, merciful to non-Chinese people like me.

And I feel all right, I really do. Better than I ever expected. I don't even get the sick feeling. Or, at least, not until the end of the meal, when the waitress brings a silver tray with three gourmet fortune cookies, a cruel punch line to a stupid, stupid joke.

That night, I dream of elfin women with sesame-brown bodies and blackbird-wing hair. I wake up bloated from last night's MSG fest. My head swims with eight-hour-old mai tai liquor.

I get up and look around. My apartment is a small, cold studio on the upper west edge of the Park. It has almost nothing in it but a bed, a very crowded desk, and a sofa I inherited from Bitsy. I shuffle to the kitchen corner and open the fridge. There's not much in there, but in the pale light that the refrigerator allows, I see tofu sandwiched between the peanut butter and half a jug of wine. See? Tofu. I could be Chinese. I swing the door shut. What do I know about China? Nothing. I have never known anyone who was Chinese. There were Chinese people back home somewhere, I guess, but no one I ever spoke to. Anyway, what does *he* know about China? I think back, looking for clues. Did we ever eat at a Chinese restaurant? I can't remember. Did we ever talk about China? No. Once, he said something about how I should leave my dirty shoes outside his door to keep the rug clean. I wonder if she does that. I wonder if she has perfect, tiny feet.

I sit down on the sofa with the newspaper, shaking my head. God, am I a racist? I must be. If I were normal, I wouldn't even think twice. What is my problem? So he's dating someone who is Chinese. So what?

The phone rings. It's Bitsy. She wants to make sure I am all right. Do I want to go shopping today? I don't. I have no money, and besides, I don't want to see rich and perfect Bitsy twice in twenty-four hours. I'll be fine, I tell her. I'll just do some work at home, thanks.

"Remember, the fact that you're both moving on is a good thing," she says before she hangs up. "We love Max, but he wasn't the one. It doesn't matter what he's doing now. You're much better off."

"Of course," I say. But I am already pulling down a box of old pictures from the closet. I stare at them for a while and then get up, walking from wall to wall. He loved me in this corner. He had me on this chair.

Shit. I've got to get out of here. I pull on some jeans and a parka and go outside. I've got to get some air. It's thirty-four degrees and sleeting slightly, but there's still air out here, and I breathe it in, along with a little marijuana I happen to have in a pipe in my coat pocket. I sort of notice that I might be in Max's neighborhood, but it's a big city. He probably won't even see me if I happen to bump into him on one of his daily runs. I sit on a bench and keep my eyes open, but he doesn't appear. Probably because he's in bed with his new Chinese girlfriend. I realize that I am being a bit of a stalker. A stoned one, even. I'd take the bus home, but I have only seventy cents in my pocket. I walk back, hike up the five flights, and put the box of photos away.

You know what's funny? My mother knew he would leave me from the start. I hated her for saying it. "He's an honest-to-God old-fashioned man," she said when she met him. "He's not Southern, but he's old-school. You're going to have to go beyond yourself to keep him. That's a tiring thing."

I ignored her. What did she know? He was such a *fun* person. We did so many *fun* things together. There was that one time he took me to dog-training school just because I said I loved puppies. I can't have one in my apartment, it's too small, but he took me there just to pet them and watch them play with balls. He made me waffles on Saturday mornings. He bought me a dress when I lost ten pounds from being in love. He told me I was strong. It made me feel stronger. He told me I was beautiful. I freaked.

And the sex. Oh, Jesus. I'd never had sex like that before, the kind of sex where I'd walk in the door and he'd close it and push me up against a wall. He told me that my skin was alabaster, that my legs were delicious, and even while he was flipping me down toward the bottom of the bed and covering me with his body, I was regretting it, because it was so good, so sweet, that I sensed, I *knew* that I'd never be able to be with anyone else without thinking of him.

Unfortunately for me, it seems I was right.

The next day, I decide to get coffee at my old special place. It's not really on the way to work. Three blocks in the wrong direction, actually, but the soy lattes, when I allow myself to have them, are good there. They make them just the way I like them. Fine, they make them that way at every Starbucks, but my special chair is there. It's a big green chair, perfect for reading the paper. It also happens to have a great view of Max's street.

It's no big deal. Not as weird as it sounds. I'm just going there to read the paper. And when I don't see him, I just go to work and forget about it. Mostly. Except for the fact that I spend the afternoon calling a few mutual friends to see if they'll say anything about the Chinese girl. They don't. Sure, I go to the coffee shop the next day. And the day after that. I start ordering Macchiatos because they have more calories, and counting them as breakfast and lunch. The other regulars begin to recognize me. Some guy asks if I live in the neighborhood. I say that I do. I point to Max's building. That's where I live, I say. I live right over there.

I start researching China. Instead of fact-checking the story I've been assigned, I read about Mao. I read about his wife, who would do any-thing to rule the country, even kill her old lovers.

I read about tea, and rice, and how monks spend years embroidering scenes on silk panels. I start dropping facts about China to other people, fun facts other people should really know. China is bordered by the Yellow Sea! 1,284,303,705 people live in China, according to the census taken this June. I call my mother back home in South Carolina and I tell her that in China, for every woman, there is 1.06 man. She tells me that I should go there. The odds sound pretty good to her.

The morning comes when I see Max. It was bound to happen—I'd been to that Starbucks every day for a month. He comes out of his building, newspaper in hand. He glances at the coffee shop and walks right toward it. I can't breathe. I look for a booth to duck behind if he comes in. He doesn't. I walk to the bathroom and stare in the mirror, trying to get my breath back.

I wish I were the graceful sort. I was trained to be. "Never chase men or buses," my mother told me. "Another one will always come along." Still, I always run after the subway, and when men go, I follow.

Nothing was black and white with Max. I left first, then I came back. In the end, he ended it all.

"I beg you," I said, "don't. I'll do anything." I was crying. I cry too much.

"I'm sorry," he said. "It's just that something's been missing for me where you're concerned. You didn't do anything, but I'm just not into this anymore. I think this other woman was my way of telling you."

So I gathered the things of mine that were around his apartment and went home to my studio. I showered. I cleaned. I felt OK about it for a few hours. Then things degenerated. I missed having someone call, wondering where I was. I missed waking up with big fingers wrapped around my ankle. He was responsible; I was a mess. He was the big rock; I was the boat crashing around in the waves. No, I was a canoe. A raft? Fuck the metaphors. I was deflated. Period.

"Please!" I cried, three days later when he finally picked up the phone. "I'm a canoe without you!"

He sighed and said it was going to be all right.

"If you knew how much I still love you," I said, "it would break your heart."

"I can't talk," he said. "I'll call you later."

So I cried and cried. But I'm a champ. My mother did not raise me to mope. I dated other people, did other things. Pottery. Cooking class. I even thought I was over it. Except that now, eighteen months later, I seem to be spending this Sunday stalking him. Literally. I'm darting in and out of stores on Broadway, ducking behind mailboxes so he doesn't see me chasing him on the street.

He gets into a cab. I flag down another.

"Follow that car!" I say. The cab driver turns all the way around and looks at me through the scratched plastic divider.

"Are you serious?" he says.

I tell him I most certainly am. I've never been so serious in my life. He shakes his head, and we follow Max all the way downtown, where he gets out in front of a shop in SoHo. There are shoes in the window, just like Bitsy told me. He goes in without looking around him. He doesn't see me. He doesn't come back out.

I take the subway home to my studio, where I

belong. That was insane, what I just did. There's no question about it. I'll stop now. I swear that I will. Right after I spend the next morning skipping work and watching a movie on TV about the Chinese opera. It's a beautiful movie, starring a flawless Chinese actress, about a man in love with another man who is in love with a woman. They all end up dead. When it's over, I am sitting on the rug surrounded by coffee cups and cigarettes. I don't even take a shower before heading out the door.

When I reach the front of the store, I observe that it is a chic little place, with handcrafted slippers made of leather and silk in the window. I hesitate. What if he's there? I could say I was just shopping. Who doesn't spend their Monday morning shopping for four-hundred-dollar flip-flops? I square my shoulders and enter. I smell lavender and shoe polish. Max is not there. There is no one there except a rich lady in a fur coat and an Asian woman by the register. It's her, of course. She must be Chinese.

She looks at me and smiles. Clearly, she has no idea who I am.

"May I help you?" she asks. She is just as Bitsy

and John described her—pretty and small, with expensive designer-looking clothes and tiny diamonds in her ears. She has a bit of an accent, from China, I guess, although it sounds more British. She must be from Hong Kong. Fun fact: occupied by the British in 1841, handed back over to the Chinese government in 1997.

I stand there like a mute idiot, staring. She grows a little concerned, walks out from behind the counter, and comes closer to me.

"Would you like to try on something?"

"Yes," I stammer. "I—I need some shoes."

"For a special dress?" she asks.

"Yes. Purple, please."

She nods and gets my size, then disappears into the back. I sit in a chair and look at the powder-blue walls, covered with rows and rows of exquisite sandals and heels and loafers. They are tiny works of art, these shoes. She returns and, to my dismay, kneels. Her long black hair falls over her shoulders as she pulls out a purple satin shoe with her manicured hands. She puts the shoe on my foot lightly. I feel her cool fingers on my skin.

"Do you like them?"

I stand up. The heels make my ankles wobble. In my sweatpants and long coat, I look like a crazy lady playing dress up.

"I have to talk to you about something," I say. She is still on her knees.

"Yes?"

She focuses on me expectantly. Her look is not completely kind. It is smart, pandering, and just slightly impatient. It is the look of a sharp woman who can probably handle anything. More than me, anyway.

"I can't afford these," I say. I put my sneakers back on.

"Well, come back when you can." She is already on to something else now, slightly dismissive.

I stop and stare for one more moment. "Take care," I say, a little more loudly than necessary. I hear my voice crack.

She nods, slightly puzzled, and then looks down again. I walk back out into the cold, bright street.

I will stop this now, this obsessive behavior. What was I thinking? I swear that I will stop. And I do. I go home, take a hot shower, and head

apologetically into work. I go out with cowork-
ers that night and don't think about Max at all. I
get plowed on vodka tonics in a glistening midtown bar with my friend from work and end
up the next morning on her sofa, missing my
stockings. I'm not going to go to that Starbucks
again, ever. No way. But then she says, "Hey, I'm
hungover. Wanna get Starbucks on the way to
work?" From her apartment, Max's Starbucks *is*
on the way, so it's fate, obviously. Just one last
time, I tell myself, as if I actually believe it.

It's pretty early, eight a.m. The guy behind
the counter doesn't even need to ask me what I
want. No one is in my chair, so I sit down, just
for a minute while my friend orders, one last
minute next to the window, where I promise I'll
never come again.

But it is fate after all, it seems. Because this
is the morning that I see them. They walk out
together, not two minutes after I sit down: he,
holding a newspaper; she, wearing a white coat
and carrying a tiny green purse. They are sol-
emn, as if they've been fighting. Her pretty face
bears a small frown.

Suddenly, with a quick, catlike movement, he

grabs her. I gasp and jump up from my chair, knocking my coffee over. It drips from the table into a steaming brown pool on the floor. People are watching and my friend calls to me, but I don't care. I smack my fist on the tinted glass.

The fighting couple doesn't notice me. They are all the way across the street. A stream of traffic buzzes between us. My palm spreads out against the thick pane as I watch, stupefied.

And then I see it. Max is crying. I've never seen him cry before, but now his face crumples. The Chinese girl watches him coolly, her expression blank. He puts one hand to her cheek, then another. She doesn't move, but he is standing there, sobbing, holding her face. He studies it desperately as if it were a map. A map he has to memorize before a long trip he will be taking.

SLEEPING WITH DOGS

I HAVE MADE MANY mistakes in my life so far, the biggest of which, according to my mother, was leaving the South. Never mind the fact that I managed to spend three good years pining after a cruel man, that I have let a once promising career in journalism go, that I drink too much and have come to like my pot. I mean, I wouldn't say that I'm an addict, but try and take it away, and swear to God, I'll bite you like a snake.

Anyway, I'm back now. In the South, I mean. Just for the weekend. I have come back for my sister. She is getting married today, and I will wear pink for her. Pink chiffon, to be exact, with pink shoes to match. We have always agreed to hate pink, but for Eloise, I have painted my toes to match the roses.

Eloise is very beautiful. These days, you can't always tell that she's beautiful, because she hides it in her environmental-activist way under green cargo pants and old gray sweaters. Today, however, she will look positively otherworldly. She will be a fairy in white satin.

It is ten in the morning, and I am sneaking vodka into my orange juice.

Eloise has three best friends, all men. She calls them the Brothers. They are all beautiful too, just like my sister. Before, we used to talk about how *perfect* it would be if I fell in love with one of the Brothers. We speak that way now, my sister and I. In italics. *Perfect. Cozy.* I *love* that. The Brothers, though, are far too cool for me. One is an indie rock star, but I like folk. One leads outdoorsy trips, the kind where they leave you alone for two days on an island. I do not want to be alone on an island. I kissed the third Brother once after too many beers one night, but I couldn't take it; he smelled the same as my sister, of rosemary and foreign cigarettes.

Eloise comes into my room. We are all staying together at our family's house. We have a heart-breakingly pretty house on the river—white paint, chipping black shutters, a warped piano on the screened-in porch overlooking the marsh. She asks me if I will help her with her makeup. Of *course* I will help her with her makeup. I will paint her lips pink as tulips. I will dust her cheeks the color of the inside of a shell.

My sister seems a little nervous. She is very excited about her almost husband. And why not? He is kind and handsome, and is a human-rights lawyer. His only real flaw is that he golfs too much.

Eloise doesn't even like golf. But she *loves* him.

"I hope I do OK," my sister says to me. She is wearing only her bathing suit because she has just gone swimming with the Brothers. She looks like a sea goddess.

"Why?" I ask, ready to do maid-of-honor things—drive her back to Washington, buy her a ticket to Tahiti. "Are you scared?"

Eloise smiles at me. Such a terrible smile, sort of a pitying snort and a bashful giggle and a sad grin all at one time. I deserved that, I guess. Eloise is never scared. She was not too scared to throw her body in front of oil tankers or wrecking balls. She wasn't scared to start over and commit to someone new, even though the last husband nearly killed her.

Outside, somebody yells her name.

"Gotta go," she says, and runs out.

Eloise has a lot of friends. They all met at Yale fifteen years ago. There must be thirty of them here, like a tribe. They are, almost every one of them, extraordinary. This one runs a movie studio; that one is Denver's best chef. This one makes documentary films; that one sculpts jungle animals out of sheet metal. They are so special, in fact, that a person from a magazine is here taking pictures of them as they compose songs at the piano and make soufflés and tell stories to a banjo. It is like being at the world's longest talent show. I spend my morning watching and moving from the camera as it snaps away, click click click.

The tribe, it has never really taken a shine to me.

I did not fall in love with any of the Brothers, but I have spent the last few years loving Max. He loved me back too, for a while, but then he left me for another, better woman whose voice now inhabits his answering machine. They say that he is getting married soon. I say that losing him is a good reason to be scared of pretty much everything.

Max is not at this wedding. It wouldn't make sense that he would be. His name is here, though. For some horrible reason, my sister's almost in-laws have a dog with the same name. Max. He is a big black lab, and he follows me around mercilessly, as if I am covered in meat. At night he sleeps on my bed, cuddling against my legs. This morning when I woke up, I felt the warmth and actually believed that my love had come back.

Tonight there will be one hundred people here to watch Eloise get married. There will be a band playing swing music and two bartenders and a table of perfectly quaint cupcakes. At the end, the bride and groom will ride away in the back of an old hay truck covered in flowers. I think my sister deserves better than a hay truck. I think she deserves a Rolls-Royce, a limo. A yacht, maybe. But no one asked me.

Eloise comes in again.

"Come swimming," she says.

We walk out to the dock, where some of the tribe are hanging out. One Brother plays the guitar. Other people play cards. An old roommate of my sister's who I've always thought looks like Snow White lies in the sun, wearing only bikini bottoms.

"Hey!" A Brother looks at me. "Ready for the firing squad?"

"No," I say.

"Absolutely," says Eloise, before doing a cannonball.

"It's our little bachelorette bridesmaid," he says to me. "So, you on the prowl tonight?"

"'On the prowl'?" Snow White scoffs. "Please. Did you get a ride here in the fucking old-school preppy misogynist express?"

I put my toe in the water and say nothing. It's early-spring water. Freezing. I don't know how my sister has not died of hypothermia yet.

"Jump *in!*" she says, tugging at my feet.

"Too *cold*," I say.

Suddenly I feel four sets of hands on my back, a whole family of fingers, and all at once I am immersed. It's even colder than I thought. I come up and swear and sputter and cough. Everyone laughs. I taste snot. The magazine person takes a picture.

"*Cozy!*" Eloise says, swimming laps around me.

And then Eloise disappears for the rest of the afternoon. It's not the kind of wedding in which we have to go together to the beauty parlor or anything, so I smoke a joint and then curl up for a nap. It's nice to nap after a joint, because instead of dreaming about all the wrong things, I just dream about roast turkey and seltzer water. The dog lies with me until I wake up an hour later in a panic. I am supposed to do the makeup. I get up and run to my sister's room, which is now packed with women messing and fussing and pulling. Eloise looks like a movie star. Her hair is up and her eyes are lined black and her cheeks are pink and her lips are sticky with gloss. There's nothing left for me to do but stand there.

"Sorry," I say.

"It's OK," she says.

"You didn't wake me up."

"We forgot."

"Oh." I am still a little stoned. I stand there some more.

Snow White gives me some champagne, then turns back to the activity. "Has anyone set out your dress, Weez?" she asks.

"Oh, perfect. You can get my dress ready," Eloise says. "That's what you can do."

"OK," I say. "Where is it?"

"In the car."

"Your car?"

"His car."

"The red one?"

"The blue one."

"In the back?"

"Parked in front."

"But the dress is in the back?"

"Check it out!" says a Brother triumphantly. It's the outdoorsy one. He comes in and dumps a cloud of white satin on the bed and grins. Everyone hoots, as if he has done something amazing.

"Maybe you should go get ready," Eloise says.

I refill my champagne glass and shuffle back to my room and look in the mirror. I look like shit. I've gained weight from the new antidepressants, and my nose is sunburned. I have circles under my eyes. I take off my clothes and wrap myself in a towel, then go out on the porch with my drink. It feels good to be naked. Naked and ready to screw. I could screw someone tonight. For a while now I have been screwing, trying to get the sadness out of my brain. I have been screwing my friends and my not-friends and anything in between. It's absurd, all the screwing, because it doesn't even begin to help. The dog isn't screwable, but he's been the best sleeping partner yet.

Eloise pokes her head out a window and yells at me to shower. I pour myself a glass of vodka and do what she says. It feels good to stand under the water, watching it pool around my feet. I have pretty nice feet. My toes look good in pink. I get out and pull my hair up. I'm feeling a little happier now. At least I can do my own makeup. I spread it on, sorority-girl style, and then put on my dress. I pull my silky skirt up over my head so only the crinoline is showing. I do a curtsy in the mirror. La-dee-da-dee-da. I've got to be the world's most screwable bridesmaid.

"Hey," one of the Brothers says.

I drop my dress. "What are you doing in here?"

"Your sister told me to tell you to hurry."

I look at him. He is the outdoorsy one. I always liked him the best.

"Do you want a blow job?" I ask.

"Um…"

"What are you doing?" Eloise asks, coming in behind him. The outdoorsy Brother bolts, terrified.

"I am the world's most screwable brides-maid," I say.

"Are you drunk?"

"No."

"Jesus, Sarah. You look like a clown." She takes a washcloth and rubs the makeup off my face, then starts over.

"Sorry."

"It's OK."

"I'll be good."

"I'm not worried."

"There's a lot wrong with me," I say.

"I know," she says. "But right now you have to be in a wedding."

I tell her I'm sorry again, which she waves off. I am sort of always sorry. I am sorry for being drunk on her wedding day and for not being good enough for Max and for not being smart enough for her friends and for breaking her toe with a hockey stick when I was twelve. God, I am sorry. I am sorry for so many things that I should go outside and swim to Cuba.

"That's better," she says, finishing my face.

"Thank you," I say. She tries to hug me, but I shrug her off. I hate girl hugs. She laughs and goes away.

I'm ready now, but I have nothing to do, so I sit on the bed. One more hit of pot won't hurt. I can hear laughing down the hall. I should probably go in there. I should help Eloise put her dress on and tell her how pretty she is. I should do a lot of things. I put the pipe away and stand up and yell for the dog, but he's already gone. Someone calls my name, and I go back into the wedding room where my sister is, only it's not my sister anymore but somebody else's almost-wife.

"You look pretty," I tell her.

"Thanks," she says. The Brothers are staring at me. Obviously they've been talking, and now they hate me. Go ahead and hate me, Brothers. Whatever. I'm wearing pink.

"Everyone's here," Eloise says.

"Really?" I go to the window and look down. She's right. There are rows of people sitting and waiting. "Shit." All of a sudden the pot is making me terrified, and I'm starting to sweat. *"Scary."*

"Yeah," Eloise says, though it's obvious that she is not nervous at all. Everyone leaves and it's just us in the room, waiting for someone to tell us when it's time to go. The air is heavy, and I feel the weight of these minutes, as if maybe there's something I can do or say that will make any difference to anyone.

"This is weird," I say.

"I know," she says.

"Do you remember," I say, "that time I broke your toe with a hockey stick?"

"Yes," she says. "That sucked."

"Sorry about that."

"You are always too sorry," she says.

"It was pretty bad, though," I say. "I sort of did it on purpose."

"Move *on*," she says, and now I am even sorrier, because Eloise is mad at me. She turns and goes back to the window to look out at her future, and I think about how much I love my sister, how amazing and strong and loyal she is, and how scared I am that she is going to leave me, and how if I were anything like her, I'd tell her all of this, every word, with no italics at all.

My father knocks on the door.

"I really don't want to go first," I say.

Eloise turns around and looks at me. "You'll be all right," she says. She wraps her arms around me and hugs me, and for once, I let her. Then she opens the door and pushes me forward, because everyone is waiting for me to begin.

SNOW IN BANGLADESH

IAN IS LEAVING. The dinner plates are on the table, there is chocolate cake next to the bed. I was asleep, but now I'm awake and it's not light yet. The clock glows two a.m.

"I have a meeting first thing," he says to the question I didn't ask. He looks out the window. "It's raining cats and dogs out there."

"Do you have an umbrella?" I say.

"I'll get a cab," he says.

"A cab is not the same as an umbrella," I say. "Take one from the hallway. The purple one. You can give it to me later."

"All right." He kisses me, but it's an I'm-gone-already kiss. He has meetings. He has cats and dogs. I go under the covers and pretend to go back to sleep.

"Adios," he says. *Adios* is Ian's signature thing. They have all had signature things, but *adios* is by far the most annoying. *Adios* is why I should never let him into my house and give him cake. I always do anyway. When I hear the door shut, I get up to do the dishes. The umbrella hangs, untaken, in the hallway, winking from its wooden peg.

THE CAMELLIAS have a saying about courting: men are pots. For the best meal, keep all the burners going on your stove.

My mother says it all the time; she said it when I broke up with Max and when I came alone to my sister's wedding. *Keep the burners going. More pots, more pots.* I've never asked her exactly what she means by this, but I'm guessing the meal that ends up on your table is a husband, warm and big and ready to eat.

But I am twenty-nine, and thus far, there have been many pots.

There was the Boss. It was during my first job out of school at a publishing house. I was twenty-two and was paid $18,450 a year to shuffle through dead books and xerox. One editor requested me for all his jobs.

"No one organizes my files like you do," he told me. For some reason, I took this as a compliment. He kept me at the office late and ordered us take-out food. We finally had sex under a conference table after too much beef pho. *Cozy,* I thought. I had fortune-cookie crumbs all over my back.

"I love you awful," he said.

"Me too," I said.

Then one dark morning, I got a memo. Just to me.

Please stop fraternizing with your married superiors. This is your final warning.

"What?" I said. This doesn't happen to smart girls. I'd written an honors thesis on Flannery O'Connor and the dangers of lupus! I ran into his office and looked and saw a big gold ring I'd never laid eyes on before, heavy on his finger.

"Oh, baby," he said.

Sorry, baby. Sorry, sorry.

MAX WAS the next one. As much as I try to explain what happened there, I can't seem to tell it correctly. I'll just lean on the Camellia clichés and say that Max was my biggest, boiliest pot, and he burned the hell out of me.

ONE OF my favorite ones was Gabe. We met in Europe while I was traveling with friends the summer after college. We had matching Converse tennis shoes! Whatever. We went around together, hostel to hostel. Instead of touring, our thing was to buy cheap wine and play cards at famous places. Gin rummy at the duomo. Euchre at the Louvre. We never ran out of things to talk about. He was crazy; he made me dye his hair blue in Rome. Once, he made me laugh so hard I peed.

We had to separate eventually. He had a little

dead grandmother money; I had a maxed out American Express card to pay. On the last night, we splurged on a sleeper car. There were other people in the car, some Germans we met. Everyone was sleeping around us, but it was like we were sentenced to die the next day or something. We couldn't keep our hands off each other. We made love with all those people around, pressed silent and tight as praying hands. It was hot. The windows were open, and the full moon shone bright, reflecting off Gabe's slick, young shoulder. Outside, the Amalfi Coast rushed by, soft blues and purples streaming past us in van Gogh strokes. It was so perfect that sometimes I wonder if I dreamed it, but I know this was real because dreams, I always eventually forget.

MOM IS WORRIED. I need grandchildren, she says. She's already built a nursery in her house in South Carolina. On Christmas Day last year, I stumbled out, hungover, and stubbed my toe on a tiny child-size rocking chair she'd bought and set up in front of the fireplace.

"Mom," I said, taping up my foot, "are you having midgets over for dinner this year?"

She'd hung Santa stockings for my sister and me. I'd just had my first Botox injection, and my mother was hanging Santa stockings. She looked at me, pressed her lips together, gave the dog a bone wrapped in shiny green ribbon.

THE POTS, they are starting to get to me a little. I am beginning to worry about the lasting power of my stove.

Last week I realized I couldn't remember all the people I've kissed. I sat in a meeting, bored. I made a list. It filled up a page, and there were all these question marks for people whose names I couldn't remember. I laughed. Hee hee, naughty me. I began to do one for people I've slept with. My list grew past twenty. My stomach flip-flopped. It grew past twenty-five. I closed the notebook and tried to pay attention to what the man was saying about marketing trends.

I MET a really nice one at a dinner party in the apartment downstairs two years ago.

"I'm Theo," he said.

"I'm Vincent," I said, making him laugh.

We were having a good time, and it got to be three a.m., so I pulled a "walk me home" move and let him sleep at my house. We didn't do anything. He just spooned me. What I remember most clearly was that while we slept, he held my breasts gently, as if they were little baby rabbits.

I never heard from him afterward. I didn't really hang out with those people much anyway. It was OK. Then I finally saw one of them on the street, and she said, "Can you believe what happened to Theo?"

"No," I said. "What, did he get married to a model or something?"

"He was in a ski accident," she said, looking at me like I was pond scum. "They had to cut his head open like a cantaloupe to put a plate in."

"Wow," I said.

"He's not dead, though," she said, heading up the street. "Keep him in your prayers."

Prayers. OK. I don't pray, really, but I gave it a whirl. I mean, the guy wasn't dead yet.

Three months later, I ran into her on the street again.

"Hey," I said, stopping her. "How's Theo?"

"Oh." She looked away. "You didn't hear, huh?"

"Jesus."

"Yes," she said, putting her hand on my shoulder.

"You know," I said, "until now, guys just flaked out on me. Or I flaked on them. But now they're actually dying."

"That's horrible," she said, taking her hand away.

"That's what I'm telling you," I said.

MY SISTER CALLS. She recently got married for the second time. Two whole marriages, imagine that. She talks about her new house, how her and her husband's relationship instantly changed after the big ring exchange.

I tell her about Ian. He hasn't called since the cake. What should I do? Call him? Not call him? No? Yes? Maybe?

She listens distractedly. She used to be more interested; she'd ask about their backgrounds, give me steps and advice. If she met them, she'd take them aside and threaten them jokingly. "Hurt her, and I'll kill you," she'd say. She was protective. It was sweet. She never does that anymore. I ask her why.

"No offense, Tiny," she says, clearing her throat, "but what's left to protect?"

It makes me wonder sometimes where it comes from, this drive to find a new one, to think of something new to talk about, to be charming when they call. I used to think that hope was an endless well, but today on the subway my eyes met those of another overcooked woman, and I realized that, indeed, there may be a bottom to all of this.

"We'll find you a match," my married friends say when they have me over for a dinner party.

"You're so datable. We'll find you one on the Internet!" We all tromp to their study, where they keep shared books and music. They switch on the computer, and we all gather around with our glasses full of wine.

"You need a code name," my friend says.

"Sporty!" someone shouts.

Sporty is taken, the computer says. I can have Sporty76.

I have lived 10,687 days. I am the fourth in a line of family debutantes, dating back to 1904.

I am Sporty76.

THE E-MAILS start coming. A few at first, then my friends put my picture up, and I get around thirty a day.

Sexy4u likes the fact that I read.

Doctorbooy loves dogs, movies, ice cream!!

Footballguy7 can't believe he's doing this! Is he really doing this? This is crazy! But do I want to get together? Because I look so normal! Can I believe I'm doing this??

Sure, Footballguy7, I e-mail back. Meet me

Sunday in front of the museum. I'll wear a black sweater and a silver belt.

Raiders! he writes back. Rite-on!

Sunday comes. I go to the museum. I wear black and silver. I sit on the stairs out front and wait.

Wait. Wait. People go by. Men look. Could be Footballguy7. Might not be. Get cold. Go home. Pace. Go to sleep.

I SLEEP with my old boyfriend, and he talks about his new girlfriend during.

I sleep with my friend, and he talks about my other friend during.

We are all somewhere else, during.

ONE NIGHT at two a.m., I'm coming home from an Internet date. I just fended off Sexy4u, and I have to say, I'm feeling pretty proud of myself.

I'm still high from it when I get on my elevator and Gabe is there. Gabe. From Europe. From the train.

He looks at me and yelps.

"I fucking live in your building!" he says.

"No way," I say.

"Check that out," he says.

We ride the elevator back down and go have a beer at the bar around the corner. Turns out he ran through his inheritance money and is now headwaiter at a hip midtown restaurant. "Prague is beat," he says. "I left years ago. The Americans ruin everything." He has playing cards in his pocket.

"Euchre?" he says, putting them on the table.

I almost start to cry. I mean, right there in the stupid bar, I just want to start crying.

IT TURNS OUT Gabe is across the air shaft from me, one floor down. We can't see into each other's apartments exactly, but we can see each other's windows. He starts leaving notes in his window for me to read.

Hi nabor, the first one says. *It's raining out. Take umbrela.*

After a few hours, I tape one up in reply.

Thank you. Very nice.

He tapes another one up in a couple of days.

Blizard in DC. If going there, bring hat.

I get out the newspaper and scour it for something to say back.

Heat wave in Alaska, I write. *Ice caps meltng. World doomd.*

A day passes. Then:

Snow in Bangladesh, he replies. *Not doomd after all.*

I look in the paper but do not see reports of snow in Bangladesh.

You r lying, I write. *No sno there. Sno in Bhutan.*

A day passes. Then another. Whatever, I think. I leave Ian another voice mail. I make soup. Then:

Dinner tomorrow. Pick u up. Good?

I stare at it for a while, then get a clean piece of paper. I go all the way down to the bodega just to buy a red marker with a fat tip.

OK, I write. I tape it, a big square, to the window.

He comes and picks me up, wearing a blazer with jeans.

"Wow," I say.

"Yeah, man," he says. "This is a *date*." He offers me his arm and I kiss him on the cheek and we go down to the street to hail a cab.

And then: conversation stops.

All the ease that was ours in Italy and the quirkiness of our signs through the window are gone, suddenly. We are two old, stiff wooden boards. If we were a movie, it would be a sad one, one called *Before, After.* He cracks a couple of jokes that aren't funny. I tell a story a few decibels too high.

Another pause.

"You know," he finally says, "I'm done with waiting."

"Me too," I say.

"I'm moving on to bartending," he says, giving me a strange look. "I'm going to try to open my own place someday."

"Ah," I say, letting myself move toward that dark place, the place with the lady on the subway whose glance made me want to cry. Because I've got nothing left for Gabe. No story, no fresh thought. I'm boiled and strained. Put me in the freezer and let me be.

The blocks slip by in the sad quiet.

"Do you remember Italy?" he asks.

"The country?" I say.

"The train," he says. "Best night. I never forgot that. One of the best nights I ever had."

I nod and look at him and draw my finger gently across his palm, then pull it away quick because I've done that so many times on so many guys before.

I move away and look out the window. I think of my body, how far it's been since that train, like a truck, like an ugly cargo ship, and I can't. I can't do this. Not to my one still-good pot.

I'm SILENT during the rest of the ride. When we get to the restaurant, he asks for my coat.

"Actually, I have to go to the bathroom."

"You're taking your coat to the bathroom?"

"My lipstick is in the pocket."

"I'll get a table."

"Great," I say. He turns away. I waver for a second, then run for the door.

Oh, God. What am I doing? Where am I going? I could go to Cuba. I've always wanted to check out Cuba. Or to Prague, maybe.

Sory about dinner, I could write to him through the window. *Had 2 get dumplings in Prague.*

I don't know where I'm going, really. McDonald's? A bar? I guess I'll go to a bar. I pick the first one I see. It's an Irish bar that's supposed to look old, but I can tell by the shiny paneling that it's younger than the shoes I'm wearing. There's an old crusty guy two seats down illegally smoking a cigarette. Taking my cue from the miserable and lonely, I order wine and light up too.

"Hey," he says. He is old, this man. Not as old as my father, but still. His face is red, from either the sun or embarrassment or drinking. Maybe all three. He looks like a cooked tomato.

"Hi."

He glances down at his drink and then up again. "You by yourself?"

"Um…" I concentrate on the tip of my cigarette.

"It's a simple question," he says.

"Is it?" I say. I glance over at his hungry, beady eyes. "Well, OK. Then, no. I'm not. I guess."

"You guess." He shakes his head and snorts. Something flies out of his nose. "Maybe he's me," the man says. "Maybe I'm who you're with."

The bartender looks at me from his corner in a familiar manner. It takes me a minute to recognize it, but it's pity. He pities me. I give him an it's-OK-don't-worry-about-me smile and take a look at this man beside me. There will, perhaps, be a time when I think someone like this tomato man is a prize. Will it be in twenty years? Ten?

"Maybe," I say. "I mean, for right now."

"All right," he says. "Well, I guess we can talk about the weather."

I shrug, thinking of Gabe alone in the restaurant. "OK."

"It was nice out today," he says.

"It was."

"But there's been some crazy stuff happening because of this global-warming crap. People say we're not going to feel a difference in our lifetime? Bullcrap, miss. We'll all be drowning tomorrow."

"I know," I say.

"Jesus. The ice caps are melting!"

"I'm aware of that."

"There's snow in Bangladesh!"

I whip my head around so fast, I hear the bones in my neck crack. "Say that again?"

"Bangladesh," he says, holding up a newspaper and pointing to a photo of a white, crowded street. I lean in to get a look. In the picture, mothers huddle under blankets. Bewildered children catch flakes with their tongues. "There was snow there this week. It's really something."

"It is," I say. "Wow. Really."

I think about this, what this snow could mean, as I pay for my drink and the Tomato's too and slowly head back to the restaurant. It could mean we'll die tomorrow. It's true. We might all drown. But maybe, just maybe, it doesn't mean that. Maybe God just wanted to give the Bangladeshi kids a chance to have a snowball fight.

I yank the door open and look around but don't see Gabe. I don't blame him; if I'd been ditched for half an hour by a used-up rag like me, I'd leave too. But no, there he is, inexplicably still at the table. He's visibly annoyed that I've kept him waiting, and I know I've screwed up, God, I've *already* screwed this up, so I sit down and take a deep breath and tell him he's right.

"I saw it," I say.

"Saw what?" he says grimly. "A black hole? The great fucking ladies' room abyss?"

"Snow," I say. "It did snow in Bangladesh."

He looks at me, waiting, and I see that I might possibly be getting my chance back, so I start to talk. I talk about ice caps and rain and sun showers. He's still not thrilled, but he's not leaving, and I go on to tell him about Theo. I tell him about Max. I talk about stoves and umbrellas and wells of hope. He's with me now — not that he says much, just a sardonic comment and a laugh here and there — but it feels like we could go on like this for hours. Years, maybe. And really I don't know where I'm getting all of this. I don't know where it all was before. But I suppose that's why people always start with the weather. There is always something new to say.

AWAY

THE MORNING WE DRIVE up to Bitsy's house, the sky is heartbreak blue,
question-your-existence blue, the kind of blue
you look away from because, as much as you
want to find one, there's no end. We don't get
to see blues like that often—Gabe and I don't
leave the city much. We like it here, and besides,
we're poor. But it's July, and the brown, soggy
veil of summer has come to stay, clogging our
pores and pooling in our crevices. Even sex has
become an unpleasant act; afterward we roll,
annoyed, away from each other's sticky skin,
pissed off as pregnant cats. So when we got the
call from Bitsy inviting us to Vermont, we said

yes, *yes,* God, fucking yes! Get us out of this hellhole, we can't go to one more stupid alien movie for the 110 minutes of air-conditioning, can't eat one more gas-inducing cone of frozen yogurt in the name of relief.

We've packed everything. A tent, rackets, dressy clothes, bathing suits. I've never been to Vermont, but I imagine many things, from bridge in tennis whites to tapping maple syrup in fluttering flannel knickers. We carry our duffels to the rental-car office, laughing hysterically as we pull out of the garage, not just because we're stoned but because we fooled them! We haven't driven in more than a year, and now they've trusted us with one of their precious cars — a convertible, no less; Gabe sweet-talked the car lady into an upgrade. They trust us, despite our bloodshot eyes and potentially questionable intentions. They believe we'll come home safe.

Gabe and I met in a train station in Florence years ago when we were traveling after college, so on this trip we excavate our Eurorail-pass personas circa 1990s: we stock up on Red Vines and Fritos, smoke cigarettes, pass a paper cup of watery pilsner back and forth even though it's morning. Gabe made mixes for the trip, and we sing badly to the Jayhawks and the Kinks. I stick my feet out the window, waving at strangers with my toes.

When singing gets old, we turn to gossip. Up first: the How-Rich-Is-Bitsy-Really game. Gabe has never met Bitsy, and I've met her husband, John, only a few times, but I've heard stories, tales from back home of how well Bitsy's done for herself by finding a fabulously wealthy husband.

"I bet she's just Tribeca rich," Gabe says.

"No, Gabe. She's definitely private-plane rich."

"Private-plane rich? Like, a Cessna? That's not very rich."

"She said something once about John's jet."

"And he does what? Banking?"

"Hedge fund. My mom says he has, like, seventy million dollars."

"Doesn't make sense, babe. Why would anyone with a private jet want us around at their country house?"

"I don't know." I put my hand in his lap and squeeze. "Free love?"

"Seriously. Why do you think they invited us?"

I shrug, but I know exactly why she invited us: it's the code. Bitsy doesn't really like me and I don't like her. I think she is competitive, endlessly proud of her beauty, and impossible to connect with. She thinks I am uninteresting, immature, and mediocre at most things I try. Still, she's a Camellia. It means we're friends until we're dead.

Gabe and I arrive at one o'clock, and when we see the house, we don't care why we've been invited anymore. We don't care about anything; we've reached paradise. Our mouths drop as we take in the sprawling white house laced with porches, the gatehouse, the barn, the gardens. The driveway is full of gleaming station wagons and SUVs loaded down with mountain bikes and Teflon gear. It looks like the L.L.Bean parking lot, Phase Silver, the Luxury Edition.

We approach shyly, dragging our duffels in, shoes and underwear peeking through unzipped openings. "Hello?" I call. The walls are bright white, the floors are wood, painted by some artisan in a checkerboard pattern. Bitsy emerges almost instantly, wearing a gold bikini top and a sarong. Apparently, maple-tree tapping will not be happening today.

"Hello, hello!" she says, hugging us lightly. "Welcome!" We thank her, standing awkwardly in her designer hallway.

"Just drop your bags there," she says. "Rosa'll take them up." Gabe and I look at each other. Bitsy has a Rosa? She turns and leads us around, showing us the pool, where other attractive couples lounge and chat, the gargantuan kitchen, the living room with the stone fireplace and windows overlooking a huge green field.

"This is nice, Bitsy," I say, and she nods, as if to say, *Of course it is.*

"Stay there," she says. "Let me get you some wine." She turns briskly and trots away. We remain obediently rooted to our spots.

"Looks like Ralph Lauren whacked off in here," Gabe finally whispers, and I snort with laughter. Bitsy returns with two chilled glasses, looking at us suspiciously.

"It's an old house," Bitsy says. "It was built in the mid-eighteenth century. I'd take a new Hamptons house any day, but John loves this place." She leads us up the stairs to a crisp bedroom of yellow and white. "This is the Jasmine Room," Bitsy says.

"Wow," I say, "it actually *smells* like jasmine in here."

"Of course, Sarah," Bitsy says, giving me a withering look. "Every bedroom's named for a flower, and then I make it smell that way with either fresh flowers or candles or fresh potpourri. There's the Jasmine Room, the Lavender Room, the Lily Room. We've got the Honeysuckle Room. John loves it."

"Dude," Gabe says.

"Come on down to the pool when you're ready," Bitsy says, turning to go.

As soon as she closes the door, we giggle again. We are still a little high. "The Jasmine Room? The fucking Jasmine Room? Where *are* we, babe?" Gabe says, pointing to our duffels. "Holy shit. Rosa brought our bags!" He takes off his shirt and pants, climbs on the bed naked, and starts jumping.

"Stop it!" I say, but I'm laughing too hard to make him. He looks like a monkey.

"It's an *old house!*" he says, doing a Bitsy. "I'd take the Hamptons *any day!*"

"Gabe!"

With an impressive leap, he jumps off the bed and throws the shutters open.

"I AM YERTLE THE TURTLE IN THE JASMINE ROOM!" he cries. "I AM KING OF ALL I CAN—oh, shit."

"What?"

"Bitsy's down there."

"Where?" I peek out. Below, her lovely back is retreating.

"She was looking up."

"Did she see you?" We look at each other, momentarily horrified, and then start laughing again.

"She might've."

"Shit."

"I know."

"Let's go."

We pull on our bathing suits and tiptoe down the stairs sheepishly. At the pool Bitsy is pouring wine. She is pleasant and does not mention seeing my boyfriend's penis. We meet a blond couple from Georgetown and a brunette couple from Connecticut. Seth, Bitsy's brother, is on a lounge chair next to a waif of a girlfriend. He's a doctor now, and has become better-looking with age. It's too bad. Back home, he was the sort of boy who really deserved to grow up fat.

"Hi," I say.

"Hey, Walters," he says, not getting up.

I make conversation for a while, an act I find oddly simple and pleasant. It's as if we've stepped into an insulated world completely away from our everyday New York annoyances, such as looming American Express bills and the recent derailment on the N Line. Here, talk is of picking blueberries for cobblers. Villas in Italy. Hiring good help.

"I love that!" the Georgetown wife keeps saying about items Bitsy is wearing. "It's so *cute!*"

John, Bitsy's husband, has been missing, but after an hour he steps out of the garden. He's fifteen years older than us but still is an impressive-looking man: broad shoulders, distinguished graying hair. He's not handsome, but there is something in his face that is dark. A little scary, maybe. He's wearing a white polo shirt and a belt decorated with pink lobsters. He gives me a kiss and shakes Gabe's hand.

"Thank you for having us," I say.

"My pleasure," John says.

"This place is amazing, man," Gabe says.

John smiles coolly. I watch him slowly take in Gabe: his tattoos, his ironically plaid fifties swimsuit, his dyed blue-black hair. "Well, money," John says. "It does make things pleasant."

We swim and lounge and chat. The Georgetown couple is looking for a new town house. Seth's radiology practice back in Charleston is taking off; everyone's getting cancer, which is great for business. The Connecticut couple tells us they're trying to have kids, a statement that immediately causes me to picture them screwing frantically. Gabe has two more beers and, citing too much sun, goes up for a nap.

I go into the kitchen to find Bitsy. She's making dip, a sight I find vaguely surprising. "I never took you for a cook," I say.

"I do it for John," she says. "But mostly I've only mastered chopping. Rosa does the rest."

"How lovely," I say.

"So," she says, leaning forward and lowering her voice, "Gabe seems nice."

"He's great," I say. "I love him."

"That's important," she says. "How is the sex?"

In terms of manners, it's acceptable for Camellias to speak freely of sex. Southern girls are highly sexual beings; in high school, we quietly swapped the secrets to a good blow job (lips covering teeth, an abundance of thick saliva) and the names of doctors who wouldn't tell our mothers about our birth-control prescriptions. Speaking of money is distasteful. Talking about health, dull. But sex, when approached with a decent amount of grace and understanding, is always fair game.

"It's nice," I say. "It's good."

"That doesn't sound that good," she says.

"Why, how is the sex between you and John?" I imagine sex with John to be, pardon the pun, pretty stiff. I mean, the guy has the sense of humor of a pool rake. And then there are those lobsters. It doesn't matter. He's polite and worth seventy million dollars.

"It's nice," she says, flipping her carefully caramel-colored hair over her shoulder. "It's fine."

"Fine?"

"Well, he learns from the other women. So that keeps things interesting." She says this casually, as if she is back outside talking about the hue of her sandals.

"What other—"

"It's normal, Sarah." She meets my eyes, and I see that she is exasperated and sad. "You try being married for a while."

"I'm sorry," I say, putting my hand on her arm.

Bitsy's inner emotional windshield wiper clears her face back into placid beauty, and she whips her arm away. I look around. Did that just happen?

"Don't be. Anyway, yes, our sex is mediocre. Shitty, even. But we're married. It's supposed to be shitty. You, though, are not supposed to be having shitty sex."

"I didn't say sex with Gabe was shitty. You did."

"Sure," Bitsy says, treating me to a dazzling smile. "Here. You must be starving. Have a carrot."

Just to prove Bitsy wrong, after eating my carrot I go upstairs and have sex with Gabe.

It's not shitty, actually. First he gets on top and I come, then we flip-flop and he shudders after a few minutes of my lap dancer–esque bouncing. Not shitty. Not shitty at all.

"Wow," Gabe says. He rubs my back, and I look at him. He is cute, my Gabe. Brown eyes, soft skin. A little skinny, but I overlook it because he is so good for me. "Finally, some decent sex."

"What? We always have decent sex."

"Not this summer. It's too hot. We've been having survival sex. Babe, your brain's been off in Iceland."

"Hmmmm." I decide to let that bit of truth drift.

"I love vacation."

"It's great, isn't it?"

"Someday we should get a house like this."

"Maybe," I say. Gabe is always talking about

the *we-shoulds*. *We should* move in together. *We should* have kids someday. He seems very sure about the future, but "maybe" is pretty much all I can manage. I'm not sure why this is, because I know I'll never find anyone kinder, but when I think of Gabe and myself ten years down the road, all I see is a blur.

"Can we smoke a little more pot?" I ask. "I can't talk to these people sober."

He's quiet for a moment, and my heart pounds. Can he tell what I'm thinking? What the hell is wrong with me? Why am I in Iceland? But then I realize that he's just taking a hit. He blows it out and hands me his pipe. I take it, feeling the blood rush back into my heart.

"Sure, babe," he says. "And don't worry. I get you. It's us against them, sweetie. We're a different breed."

Dinner is early, and we eat as if locusts are coming. We eat ribs, and roast chicken with crisp herb-rubbed skin, and pork sausage with fresh fennel. We eat potato salad made from homemade mayonnaise and smoked bacon, and corkscrew pasta salad with fresh basil and pine nuts, and tender green salad picked from the garden, and sweet beets that stain our mouths jewel-red. Afterward, we sit in the garden, bloated, on plush-pillowed couches. We rub our bellies and look glassy-eyed at one another in the waning afternoon light.

"This is so fantastic," Seth says. The waif giggles. I have yet to hear her speak.

"The good life," the Georgetown husband says.

"So, Gabe," Bitsy says, draping her perfect arms over her head, "tell me about the peace corps. It sounds fascinating."

"It was. Ecuador is a fucking amazing country."

"Really." She swivels her head toward him, looking at his face as if he is the Oracle of Delphi.

"Fuck yeah," Gabe says. "It was so enlightening, being isolated like that. I became a totally different person."

"Wait, stop, stop, stop!" I laugh.

The previously pleasant din of conversation ceases as all eyes rest on me.

"Gabe!" I say. "You weren't isolated. You had an apartment in Quito. With cable."

"What's wrong with her wanting to hear about the peace corps?" Gabe asks. "I'd like it if sometimes you would listen more to my stories about Quito."

"What the hell, Gabe? I listen all the—"

"OK, kids," Seth breaks in authoritatively. It takes physical effort, but I manage not to roll my eyes.

"Sorry," I say to make up for the awkward silence. I give Gabe a goofy kiss and a hug and am rewarded with relieved smiles around the circle.

Bitsy sits up. "Shall we walk?" she asks the air. I sigh. I am full and sleepy and annoyed. I do not want to walk. I want to sit on this daybed and look at the mountains and drink and pout.

"I'm out," I say.

"Really?" Gabe says.

"Really."

Bitsy rises. The others follow, graceful as spring trees. "Just a little hike to the waterfall."

I shake my head.

"No, thanks."

"Do you mind if I go, babe?" Gabe says.

"Nope."

"Really?"

"I don't care."

"It's just a walk, Sarah," Bitsy says. "I promise you won't get eaten by bears."

"I just feel like sitting here," I say. "Don't worry, Gabe. I'll be fine."

"OK," he says hesitantly. He leans over and kisses me. "Are you sure you're OK?" he whispers.

"Fine, fine." I wave him off.

"See you later, hotness."

"See you," I say.

They walk off together down the path. I listen to their fading voices until all I hear are the leaves in the wind. The garden, which I'd hoped would feel peaceful, feels sad. Seriously, what is wrong with me? Why don't I care about Gabe's Quito stories? Why aren't I richer? And prettier? And better? After a few minutes I get up and go inside the house. I look at Bitsy's antiques and sofas and books. I go upstairs to Bitsy and John's room. Their bed is made nicely, a pretty coverlet decorated with green sprays of honeysuckle that match the green walls. I look at their wedding photos, their books, their alarm clock. Their bedside-table drawer. The carved wooden box under their bed containing the vibrator and the bottle of Astroglide. Bitsy's closet. Bitsy's medicine cabinet—

"Hi."

I turn, Klonopin bottle in hand. It's John, Bitsy's frightening-in-a-nice-way husband.

"Hey, John." I look down. "Hi."

"Need some aspirin?"

"John..." Why lie? What can John do to me? "I was actually checking out Bitsy's stash."

John's face remains blank for a moment, then lights up into a laugh. He laughs so hard that he doubles over. I'm not sure he should be laughing this hard, but maybe I am really that funny.

"You're a very honest person," he finally says.

"Sometimes." For show, I pop a Klonopin and put the bottle back in the cabinet. "Why aren't you walking?" I ask.

"Me?" John adjusts his glasses. "No. I hate hiking. Pointless activity. I said I was going back to do dishes. During the day, when she leads one of these expeditions, I always say I'm going to the hardware store, but then I just sit around here, reading. Bitsy doesn't even notice that I haven't bought anything."

"That's hilarious," I lie. I take a seat on a chintz-covered chair by the fireplace. John sits down on his bed. He leans forward and puts his elbows on his knees. He seems not at all uncomfortable conversing with a strange woman in his bedroom.

"So." He looks at me quizzically. "You and Bitsy grew up together."

"Yup." Klonopin hits you fast. I can feel my edges dissolve.

"You're very different, though."

"I know, I know. She's big on the manners thing. I sort of dropped out of the debutante scene."

"Oh, I'd say you have some Southern twang to you."

"Oh, yeah," I say, slumping into the chair. "I ooze charm."

He looks out the window. "Sarah," he says, "would you like to see the secret attic room?"

"There's a secret room?" I say, perking up. "Really?"

"Yes. The original owners of this house were Tories, and before and during the Revolutionary War, they built a secret room to hide a young British couple who were teaching here in the village. They lived there for a year before escaping in the middle of the night."

"How awesome!" I say, then, "I mean, how amazing that this house has such historical significance."

"You don't have any marijuana, do you?" John asks.

"Yeah," I say, relieved. "Sure. Hang on." I jump up and he follows me to the Jasmine Room, which, after seeing Honeysuckle, I have to say looks pretty dinky. I dig the pipe out of the pocket of Gabe's shorts. "I didn't know you smoked."

"I don't often. Bitsy doesn't like drugs in the house. But I dabble."

"Well, here it is," I say, holding up the pipe and the lighter. "Dabble away."

"Let's go to the room first. It's really quite

amazing." We go down the hall to a small, musty study that wasn't included on the Bitsy intro tour. The shelves are lined with old leather-bound books.

"No way," I say.

"Way," John says, smiling. He walks to one of the shelves, puts his fingers in a small groove, and pulls the shelf open to reveal a door. It actually wouldn't make a great hiding place at all today if angry Colonial rebels were trying to find and kill you; a slide-away door in a dusty library is the first place any cinematically educated stalker would look.

He opens the door, and we climb a tiny spiral staircase that leads up to a good-size room — bigger than the Jasmine Room, anyway. It's empty and bright even in the waning light, with one huge floor-to-ceiling window. With a swift, strong movement, John opens it, letting in a rush of delicious, grassy air. He sits, dangling his legs out. He has irritatingly nice shoulders, especially for a forty-five-year-old husband of a loyal debutante sister.

"Pot, please," he says.

I sit gingerly, take a small hit, and hand it to

him. He lights it and inhales deeply, once, twice, three times. The guy's on a mission, I think to myself.

"Thanks," he says, handing it back to me.

"No problem."

We sit silently, looking out at the green grass, now misting over in twilight. Below us, lightning bugs weave through the flowers in the garden. Swallows rush, chattering, through the trees.

"I love it up here," John says. "Aside from the roof, it's the highest spot in the house."

"Yertle the Turtle," I say. "King of all you can see."

He laughs, and I feel proud. Bitsy may think I am mediocre, but I believe that it is a real accomplishment to make someone like John laugh.

"You know that story, don't you?" I ask.

"Of course," he says. "Seuss was a genius. A wonderful cautionary tale for someone of my ilk."

"You and your ilk." I close my eyes and listen to the leaves rustle, a ghost ballroom humming with a thousand dancing silk skirts. I am aware of a familiar, comforting pressure, and I realize that John is holding my hand. He's not coming on to me, or it doesn't feel like he is; it's just what he's doing now, in this moment, because we are alone in the secret room where, two hundred or whatever years ago, two lovers hid to save their own lives.

"You're fascinating," he says.

All right. So maybe he is coming on to me.

"I'm stoned," I say.

"Sarah," he says.

"*You're* stoned."

"Sarah."

"No."

"Look at me for a second."

"No." I don't look. I won't look. And then I do look, and he kisses me, and it's wonderful. It's the moth plantation I've been searching for since Max shot my chest cavity full of numbing cream; it's the pulsing, rushing, horrible sweetness I know Gabe can't ever give me, no matter how kind he is, how much we laugh, or how many trips we take.

Quickly, I pull away.

"I think they're back!" I say loudly. I stumble as I get up.

John tries to steady me.

"My, you are high, aren't you?" he says, standing.

I look at his face again, but he's gone now; things have gotten too messy and he's stepped conveniently out of this. I feel bad for Bitsy. He is not a nice man.

"That's a terrible belt," I tell him. Then I go downstairs.

As it happens, they're not back, but I can hear them approaching, and I sit down on the daybed in the garden as if I've done absolutely nothing since they've been gone. And really, I haven't, so what the hell. But I have, I feel it when Gabe comes back, smiling and trusting, when he kisses me hello.

"Still here?" Bitsy says. "Is John with you?"

I shake my head.

"John!" she calls, heading quickly into the house. "Honey! Where are you? Darling? Can I make you a martini?"

"Move," Gabe says, poaching my pillows. I scoot over and lean into all his goodness.

"How was your walk?" I say.

"Crazy," he says. "The people from George-town are *Republicans,* babe. And I had to tell that Connecticut girl who the Ramones were. Then she was, like, 'Wow! We should go see them play sometime!' Sad," he said, shaking his head.

"Sad," I say. The others are inside now. Through the open window, I can hear people talking about nightcaps and bed.

"We should go in there," I say.

"Screw it," he says. We lie back and look at the stars that are popping out now, defiantly freckling the sky. "Those people are douche bags. I wish we had the pot."

"I've got it," I say, handing him the pipe.

"Oh," he says. He looks at me strangely. "Babe," he says tonelessly, "what'd you do here?"

"I'm sorry," I say. "It wasn't on purpose." I feel tears well in my eyes.

"I just packed this, you stoner!" He laughs easily—so easily!—and puts it in his pocket. "Hey," he whispers, "screw the Jasmine Room. I mean, look at these fucking stars. We should sleep out here. Want to?"

I nod, and Gabe wraps his arms around me. He is snoring within minutes, because people who don't lie, sleep. Me, I've got at least six hours to get through until the sun sneaks back up again. When it does, I'll wake him with a kiss. We'll sneak away in the gray dawn light. Take our bags. Leave a note. No one will even notice we're gone.

FOURTEEN YEARS
AFTER GEORGIA

TWO HOURS BEFORE the Ravenels' Christmas party, my mother pulled out her dress. She laid it, carefully, on the bed, inspected it for stains, and ironed the back, still wrinkled from an earlier event. She took a long bath and shaved her legs. She rubbed her limbs with lotion that smelled like rose water. She put on her robe and blew her hair out with a big prickly brush so it was shiny and fluffy and straight.

My father came in to retrieve his glasses. "Wow," he said, looking over at my mother in her robe, her graying hair in hot flight. He glanced at his own reflection, patted his stomach, tucked in his shirt, and shuffled out. When she turned off the hair dryer, my mother could hear my father turning on the computer in the next room. Computer games were his latest hobby; he'd sit for hours in front of the monitor, blowing things up on the glowing blue screen.

My mother pulled on her dress, zipped up the back, and began applying her makeup. She started with base, then darkened her eyes, brushed pink onto her cheeks, and put on red lipstick. As she applied a layer of lip gloss, she heard the phone.

"Eliza!" my father yelled. "I'm about to win! Help! Can you get that?"

My mother calmly applied one last coat of gloss, then answered the phone on the fourth ring.

"Hello."

"Eliza, it's Louisa."

My mother cradled the phone to her shoulder and looked at herself in the mirror as she crammed her toes into a web of straps.

"Can you and Henry pick up a couple of bottles of white wine? We have red, but I need white."

"Of course," my mother said, teetering on the carpet in front of the mirror. Was she too old for these heels?

"Oh—and I wanted to tell you—Henry's not on the phone, is he?"

My mother sat on the bed. "No. Well, wait. HEEENRREEEE? ARE YOU—oh, no. He's in the next room."

"OK. I just want to tell you—"

"WHAT, SWEETHEART?" My father yelled from in front of the computer.

"—that Georgia's not coming tonight."

My mother paused. "Really."

"I just wanted to let you know because you asked."

"Ah. Well."

"It's too bad. She's always a fun addition. And you two used to be so close."

"It doesn't matter," my mother said, sitting on the bed. "Did she…mention why she can't come?"

"No. Well. Something about a date. You know Georgia."

"Eliza?" my father called.

"NOTHING." My mother breathed out

harshly and then put the phone back to her ear. "All right," she said, staring at her overdressed feet. "See y'all in a bit, then."

"See you."

My mother hung up the phone and looked at it for a moment. She stood in front of the mirror and twirled, slowly, one last time. She opened her stocking drawer, where she kept an old pack of cigarettes, lit one, and then fell back, fully dressed, on her bed. She smoked it all the way down to the filter. When she was done, she rose and walked to the next room, where my father was sitting. He stopped the game, put out his arms. She paused, smiled, and kissed him. Then they went to the party by themselves.

BETWEEN LIONS

WHEN WE TURNED THIRTY, the local Camellias asked me to lunch.

I wasn't sure I wanted lunch. Lately, I'd been shying away from my Camellia sisters. Charlotte and I had fallen out of touch shortly after she engorged herself with so much heroin she almost died; it had been years now. I'd gone to dinner with Bitsy a few months before, but it wasn't something I enjoyed. I spent fifty dollars on a tiny piece of fish served on a mammoth plate while she grilled me on why I wasn't married, and then prattled on about improvements to the house in Vermont. By the end of the evening, I was depressed and starving. I ended up going home and eating an entire box of macaroni and cheese, washed down with half a bottle of old chardonnay.

Lunch.

I supposed I was ready for lunch. I had *my* life together. I'd just been hired on at a magazine, a big one with a budget and company cars. True, I was writing about moisturizer, but I had an expense account. I was dating a nice man who liked to cook me dinner. I was exercising three times a week and buying organic broccoli. For some reason, the broccoli meant the most to me. I barely ever ate it—organic vegetables wilt almost instantly—but putting the six-dollar stalks in the crisper made me feel as if I'd made it.

Charlotte called on a Tuesday to tell me about this happening. I remember the day because Tuesday is Product Drop Day, meaning there is an onslaught of new beauty products to review. My desk was covered with lotions and skin-saving serum. I don't look at caller ID on Product Drop Day because there's too much crap everywhere; this is why I picked up the phone.

"Beauty Department," I barked.

"Sarah. Hey. It's Charlotte." Her rich Southern voice spilled into my ear. It was startling. I lost my accent years ago.

"Charlotte. Hi! Hello!" I felt a surge of annoyance, followed by another of guilt. "How are you? Are you OK?"

She laughed. "I'm OK, Sarah. What, you think I'd call you if I was high?"

"No. I didn't mean that. Of course not."

"Be honest. You sort of meant that."

"I didn't."

"Whatever. How's the magazine?"

"It's good. I cover the beauty news. You know, it's OK. I'm trying to work toward features, maybe get them to do some more serious—"

"Bitsy wants to have lunch," Charlotte interrupted. "Can you come?"

"Let me look at my calendar and call you back."

"How about Friday?"

"Um, maybe. There's this editorial meeting…"

"Don't bullshit me, Sarah. I can tell when you're lying."

"OK," I said. "Friday."

"Good. We'll all meet between the lions."

I agreed to the plan and hung up, already trying to figure out how to break it.

I break plans. Gabe was used to this. In fact, the night after that phone call, I tried to get out of dinner plans, citing fatigue. But the man was resilient.

"I bought steaks," he said. "You're coming."

I was two hours late when I knocked on his door. He opened it, smiling.

"Hi," I said.

"Hey, babe."

"Hi. Sorry I'm late."

"No problem. You're always late."

"I know. I'm sorry."

"It's OK!" He smiled and kissed me. I stiffened. Lately, I didn't like kissing Gabe. I really, really wished that I did, but something about the way his tongue darted in and out of my mouth made me think of salamanders. He was so fantastic in every other way that I was trying to work on it.

"Martini?" he asked.

Exactly.

"So what's happening?" he said cheerfully.

"I dunno. Product Drop. There's some kind of new cellulite drug they want me to care about."

"You're brilliant. This is just a transitional phase. You won't always have to write this bullshit."

I smiled. Gabe was a saint. He knew about martinis, and that I don't like to talk in the morning, and how I take my grits — a little butter, lots of salt. He made strong coffee. I was trying my hardest not to lose him.

"Thanks," I said. "You're brilliant too."

"I know it," he said. "Just waiting for everyone else to find out." He forced a kiss on me. "What else happened?"

"I got a call from an old friend from home today. Charlotte. She and Bitsy want to get together for lunch."

"The cokehead? Or, wait, was it H?"

I'd forgotten that I'd told him about her. I always thought of myself as a loyal person, but it seemed I'd told everyone about Charlotte's follies.

"Well, she says she's not anymore."

"You said she kept relapsing."

"She's my friend, Gabe. Anyway, I have to go. She's a Camell—" I stopped myself. Gabe was raised in New Jersey. He didn't understand the inexplicable powers of the Camellia Society.

"She's a friend from home. I have to see her."

"You don't *have* to do anything."

"Gabe, fuck off about this. Something's up. I need to go."

The look on his face was one of a drowning kitten. Immediately, I felt like Satan. I'd waited for a man this good my whole life, and boom! Here he was. But no one ever told me the part about love repelling as much as it intoxicates.

I am so fucked up.

"I'm sorry." I kissed him, forcing myself not to pull away when his tongue slid messily against my lips.

"I love you, babe," he said.

"I know," I said, pulling away and finishing my drink. "Same here."

Before we fell out of touch, Charlotte and I always met between the large carved stone lions on the steps of the public library on Fifth Avenue at 42nd Street. We, of course, were not the first people to choose the lions as a meeting place. Everyone meets between the lions: ladies who lunch, bankers, people meeting up after traveling from faraway lands. It was my habit to get to the lions at least ten minutes early to watch. The afternoon we met for lunch was a beautiful, warm day at the beginning of October. It was crisp and lovely; a few red leaves were starting to make their fiery exits off the trees. I watched a group of Germans drape themselves over one of the lions and take pictures. One of them asked for my number, and I shrugged and gave it to him. Far away, at the other end of the steps, a chic Asian woman arrived and arrogantly lit a cigarette. Before she had time to finish, an angularly handsome man joined her. He plucked the cigarette out of her hand and laughed.

"Hey," Charlotte said. I hadn't even noticed her approach. "What are you staring at?"

"Max," I said, pointing numbly to my ex-lover. Charlotte took a moment to look and scowled as the couple walked farther away from us.

"He's still a fucker," she said.

"I know." I looked at her, blinking. The last time I'd seen Charlotte, she was pale and haggard, with short, matted hair and chipped fingernails. Now her hair was long and shiny, and she was wearing a strange but wonderful concoction of silk and chain.

"You look beautiful," I said. "Where'd you get those clothes?"

"I designed this."

"You serious?"

She laughed. "I told you I'm doing well. I've convinced some rich kids to invest in my line."

"Wow," I said, feeling frumpy and out of it. "You have anything that will look good on me?"

"It'll all look good on you, asshole," she said. She put a magazine down beside me and sat on it. "Anyway. This lunch was Bitsy's idea."

"I figured," I said.

"It's good to see you, though."

"You too," I lied. "It's been too long."

Charlotte was the first one to pick out Bitsy. It wasn't too difficult. Bitsy has a signature walk, authoritative, almost defiant, developed from years of being the prettiest in the room. She wore a linen shirt that was completely free of wrinkles. The only thing that was off was that her head had been shaved bald. It glowed in the afternoon light.

"What the hell?" Charlotte said.

Bitsy saw us, waved, and approached. I watched the strangers around us look at her, then look quickly away. One of the Germans shook his head.

"Hey, y'all," she said, smiling coolly.

"Bitsy?" I said, standing.

"Just a little bit of cancer," she said. Her sweet Southern voice rang bright. "It's not as bad as it looks. They think they've got it all with chemo. I tried a wig, but I looked like a Ken doll."

Charlotte and I were speechless. All this time and effort spent on learning manners, yet we had absolutely nothing to say. "Does it hurt?" I finally said. Charlotte treated me to a look of disgust, but Bitsy laughed, and I was happy.

"Oh, Sarah," she said, patting my head. "You've always been an idiot. But, honey, I do appreciate the thought."

*　　*　　*

We went to the Oyster Bar in the basement of Grand Central. Charlotte had taken over the conversation since my simpleton attempt, asking about doctors, symptoms. When she inquired about drugs, Bitsy, proving that cancer hadn't changed her sharper side, told Charlotte she couldn't have any.

"I wasn't going to fucking *ask,* Bitchy," Charlotte said, and Bitsy laughed, showing her perfect teeth.

"Right," she said. I watched Charlotte bristle. Out of all of us, Charlotte had always tolerated Bitsy the least. "Anyway," Bitsy said, "I've decided to move home until I get better."

"Home?" I said. "As in, South Carolina?"

"Of course," Charlotte said. "Where else would she mean?"

"I guess I just thought... well, she lives here now. With her husband."

"He'll visit," Bitsy said. "He understands."

"But your *stuff* is here now," I said. "New York is home now."

"New York? Home?" Charlotte cackled. "Sweetie. Please."

I shrugged. The waitress brought us a dozen

oysters — gray, metallic, and perfect. I picked one up, thinking of the last time I'd gone home. I felt like an alien. I'd taken Gabe, who was instantly attacked by angry mosquitoes and treated indifferently by my father. My mother was nicer, but she kept staring at his tattoos. "Did you *have* to pick a *waiter,* sweetheart?" she kept whispering loudly. I couldn't wait to leave.

"But I'm *tired* of talking about cancer," Bitsy said, bringing me back to the table. "It's boring." She looked at me. "I hear you might be getting married."

"What?" I said. "No!" The forcefulness of my answer caused them both to turn and stare. "Who said that?"

"Your mother told my mother."

"Well, no. I mean, I don't know. We haven't talked about it."

"Why not?" Bitsy said. "Isn't it sort of time?"

"No," I said.

"Why not?"

"Well," I said, "he's a bad kisser."

"Hmmmm," Bitsy said, pretty bald head shining. "Anything else?"

I took a deep breath, and the truth came

pouring out. "His breath in the morning smells like warm milk. He's so skinny I feel like I'm going to crush him when I'm on top. He doesn't like Woody Allen movies."

"Give him some Listerine," said Charlotte. "Feed him fried chicken. Tell him *Annie Hall* is a deal breaker. These are not love-killing issues."

"But the kissing?"

Bitsy looked at the bar and frowned. Max and his girl had chosen to eat here as well. He saw me, gave a casual wave, and turned away. He didn't recognize Bitsy. I ate another oyster.

"You know what I think?" Bitsy said. "You're worse off than Charlotte."

"Thanks, Bitchy," Charlotte said.

"No, I mean it," Bitsy said. "Well, Charlotte, you've had lots of problems. I mean, sweetheart, you were really screwed up for a while there. But Sarah, she's got the curse."

"What do you mean?" I said.

"You're addicted to cruel men," Bitsy said.

"That's ridiculous," I said. "Totally wrong."

"It's pretty right on, actually," Charlotte said.

"But that's terrible," I said. To my annoyance, my eyes were stinging with tears. "I mean, I must be over it." I gestured in Max's direction. "Over him, anyway. I'm sure this isn't what the Gabe thing is about. It's been years."

"Well, you know what they say in rehab," Charlotte said. "It's a process."

Charlotte got lunch. I tried to pay, but she scoffed and put down a hundred-dollar bill. I was wrong about my making it; clearly, Charlotte was the one who had found real success. She was rolling in self-made money, and would be featured in *W* and *Vogue* next month.

After lunch, we went shopping. Bitsy wanted an outfit. We didn't ask why. Charlotte suggested Orchard Street, but Bitsy was firm.

"Barneys," she said. "I hate your horrible downtown hipster shops."

So we took a cab to 60th Street, where I wandered behind the two of them, touching the fabrics and surfaces, eyed suspiciously by icy women in impeccable clothes. I didn't belong downtown, but neither was I the Barneys sort; my blazer-and-jeans combo mapped me in the nowhere in between. Charlotte picked out some things for Bitsy, dramatic pieces in bright reds and blues. We gathered together in one of the larger dressing rooms.

There is a strange familiarity between Southern women and nudity. People think that we're all about manners and being proper, but a girl from the South will take her dress off in front of you as casually as a New York girl will light up a smoke. As soon as we hit the dressing room, Bitsy shed her clothes without blinking. I tried not to stare at the violent red lines where her left breast had been.

"I want to spend a lot of John's money," she said. "I think he's having an affair."

"Really?" Charlotte asked. "Now?"

"Yup."

I didn't say anything. John and Bitsy's marriage was a gray area for me.

"Rat bastard," Charlotte said. She flipped through the price tags. "Here," she said, "try this one."

Bitsy poured herself into the red-beaded sheath Charlotte had picked. "This might do," she said.

"It looks pretty," I said.

"Don't pander to me, Sarah," Bitsy said. "I'm over pretty. I need to look like a good lay."

"I'd do you," Charlotte said.

"Thanks."

Bitsy tried on a black one next, then a blue. She settled on the red. We followed her outside to the counter.

"This would be easier, of course, if I didn't love my husband."

"You love him, huh?" Charlotte said.

"Of course. He doesn't understand me, but I still love him."

"And *he's* not cruel?" I asked. "You don't suffer from the cruel-man thing?"

"No, John's not cruel," Bitsy said. "He's terrified."

We let ourselves sit with that one for a moment. Bitsy paused in front of a mirror and looked at herself, running a manicured hand over her head. I could see that she was shaking slightly. Her eyes looked bright.

Please don't cry, I prayed to her silently. *Just please please please don't cry.*

"Did I ever tell y'all," Charlotte said suddenly, "about the only time I was in love?"

"No," Bitsy said, turning. I sighed, relieved. "Was it recently?"

"No, but it was pure love. I shot it into my arm."

"That's not true," Bitsy said, rolling her eyes.

"It is. The best fucking love ever. I've had crushes, of course. But I put that in, and my whole body was on fire. Do you know what I'm saying? I couldn't wait to get more. And if you had some right now, in your purse, I'd rip you open with my teeth to get to it."

"So why don't you go get some?" I asked. I could feel my cheeks burn. "If it's so great, why not go down to the Port Authority or Smacktown or whatever and get some right now?"

"Why don't you chase Max down?" Charlotte asked, matching my acid tone. "Why don't you stalk him? Ask him back?"

"I'd never do that."

"What, so you haven't obsessed over Max for years?" Bitsy said. "You haven't been secretly pining away, wasting your life, waiting for him to come back?"

Unexpectedly, I was furious. I am never the

mad one, but that day I was overwhelmed with uncharacteristic anger. The afternoon had taken too many turns, had teetered into the absurd. We love one another, I wanted to say. But we're always so *heartless*. Where had we learned this? Who had taught us to be so awful to ourselves?

"Why would you say that?" I said. "God, I hate you. What makes you think you can *talk* to me this way?"

"Because we're the ones who know you," Charlotte said.

I glared at her.

"Sorry," she said.

"Well," Bitsy said. "Charlotte's addicted to heroine, you're addicted to Max, and my husband's cheating on me even though I'm dying. The Camellias are really on a roll here. Our mothers would be so proud!"

Her voice rang, high-pitched and taut, bouncing off the cold, dead floor. Charlotte and I looked at her, slightly shocked. Then, together, we laughed. It was a good laugh, starting with a giggle (Bitsy), ending with a squawk (Charlotte). It went on for too long. People were staring, and we soaked it up.

"That is truly awful, Bitsy," I said, catching my breath.

"Isn't it?" Bitsy said, delighted.

Shortly after, we went our separate ways. I went back to work, and Charlotte and Bitsy left to shop some more. I think about that day often now; it was our last lunch. I broke up with Gabe a few weeks later. Bitsy died within a year. What stays with me most are not the words that were spoken but the image I have of these women—one bald and linen, one dark and silky. Arms linked, they cut a spectacular swath through the white marble hall. In New York, of course, they were nothing special to look at. Lucky for me, that's not where I'm from.

BITSY'S LIST

YOU WILL GO UP in a car. It's an old car, worn but expensive, the sort families with money keep around even though they could afford something big and shiny and new. It smells like old beer and lollipops. You'll drive up a windy road, past small towns with white churches and flea markets selling old tin buckets and rusty wagons. You won't be driving—he always drives—so you'll have plenty of time to look out the window. He won't be talking much, I think. He doesn't like to talk while he drives.

When you see the house, you probably won't believe it. Its huge whiteness sprawls across an acre of green, lush grass. He will smile at your wonder when you press your forehead against the window, looking at it. You should exclaim over the porch. You should laugh about the horses. You should be more careful about mentioning the roses. If it is May or later, they will probably be blooming, crawling optimistically up through the black iron gate.

I hope you know how to garden.

The wheels will crunch over the gravel as you park. After all the traffic, you will be happy to get there. You might expect to make love as soon as you arrive. You won't, though. There will be things to do. This used to be a farm, after all. It's not your modern country house. The water needs to be turned on. The barn needs to be checked. He will move around with purpose, doing these things, and you will climb out and watch him.

If you are smart, you will help. You will go to the car and unload bags, groceries, beer. You will find your way around the kitchen, putting bread in the bread box (by the oven, lower-left drawer) and milk in the fridge (top shelf). The thermostat is by the kitchen door. Turn it to sixty-five.

The light timer is in the living room by the oak desk. Switch it off. Open the cabinets, look at the plates and mugs. Open the freezer, where there is ice cream and, in the corner, a white container of homemade chicken stew. I wonder if you will see the stew. I wonder if you will think about how it got there.

Finally, he will come in, his cheeks flushed with cool air. You will be sitting in the living room, maybe, on the big overstuffed couch. Maybe you will be pretending to read a book. He will come and join you. If I am guessing correctly, he will immediately carry you upstairs to the bedroom. Yes. That's right, I think. He'll throw you over his shoulder and carry you up.

(This will hurt his back later. He probably won't peg the reason, but later in the day he'll have to forage for his pain pills in his toiletry bag. You should know that, if he's out, there are more in the bathroom cabinet.)

Will you kick? Will you squeal? I imagine you will. I don't even know who you are yet. Still. I think you will be younger than me. I think you will be pretty, your teeth white, your health perfect.

I think that you might squeal.

He will throw you down on the bed and cover you with kisses. He'll start with your neck. He always starts with the neck. Get comfortable. This will take a while. He'll start with your neck and then move down to your breasts. He will pause here. It's been a while since he's seen an unmarked pair of breasts. He'll unbutton your shirt, run his hand over your bra, especially if it's lacy and sheer. He loves sheer bras, not the spongy miracle bras full of padding. If you have one of those on—which you really shouldn't, they're really not very sexy—he'll most likely laugh. But if it's sheer lace, or better yet, if you're not even wearing a bra, he'll stay there, fingering your breasts, tracing patterns around the nipple with his tongue. Sometimes he uses too much tongue, lazy tongue, like a wet, limp vegetable, just sitting there. You might make a face, but don't let him see it, because that will be the end. He is sensitive. He gets frustrated easily. But if all goes well, if you arch your back just so, gasp a little in the back of your throat, he'll stay with it. He'll trace the line of your stomach, undo your belt buckle, and then—

Well.

Afterward, you will be groggy. That mid-afternoon grog that comes after a long nap in cold weather or too much sex in the daytime. You might want to loll about in bed, talking with him, reading. He won't stay for long. He is restless, and will get up after about five or ten minutes. There are things to do. He is the productive sort. This is how he came to own his firm, remember. So he will get up. For the moment, he will leave you.

This will probably make you a little annoyed. You might still lie there, to prove your point, to say, *I can lie here as long as I want; I am not her. She might have gotten up with you to work, to farm vegetables or can yams or whatever it is good wives from the South do, but I am me. I will never can yams.* But don't bother with that for too long. Trust me. He is a bit of a WASP, see. Bred from Puritans. He doesn't notice pouting. Emotion in general is an annoyance. No, if you really want to lie there, do it because you are comfortable, because you don't want to move from the fluffy pillows. It's OK to waste your time, of course. As long as it's on purpose.

If you do stay in bed, you will hear things clattering downstairs. You can hear everything going on downstairs from upstairs, so later—and this will happen only if you last—be careful when you have guests over. Don't talk about them in the house. My sister-in-law still hates me, thanks to our thin floors. I couldn't help saying it. She *does* have a flat ass. I remember she left that night, drove all the way to the city after three helpings of turkey with sage dressing. She'll probably laugh at my funeral. I can just see her now, that flat, wide ass, those ugly toes tap-tap-tap-dancing on my fresh grave.

Excuse me. I don't have to be nice anymore.

But back to you. You will need to keep yourself up. He has a wandering eye, so it's always wise to learn new skills. French cooking, maybe, or some type of massage. Keep yourself thin; make sure your hair is styled. He prefers blond highlights. As for clothes, pretty patterns are nice, but nothing too fussy. When there are other women, ignore them; they won't be a true threat unless you acknowledge them. I know this sounds impossible, but try it. There is nothing more tiresome to a man than jealousy.

Now. You will hear him rummaging. He will be getting tools, probably. Look out the window in a minute, and you can watch him doing his chores, moving the earth around, pulling this, weeding that. If you are appreciative, you will stare at his wide shoulders as they work and move. You should stare, anyway. If I were you, I'd stare for hours. He's not the most honest man, perhaps. A bit weak. A bit of a liar. But from the window, go ahead and stare at him. He's really something to see.

Sooner than later, it will be time for dinner. He will come in and say so, or, if you are still being stupidly lazy in bed, he will call up. You might take your time coming down to the kitchen. From the stairs, there's a beautiful view of a large grassy field. It can be lonely sometimes if you stand and look at it for too long. Don't. Instead, head down, where he will surely have made a fire in the woodstove. Mention it. He will be grumpy if you don't mention it. Don't gush, just a simple *It's warm in here!* will do. He'll smile and kiss you if you do that. Then he'll open the fridge and pull out the food.

There will be music on. He is always going

through some phase. Maybe on your weekend, it will be reggae or bluegrass. It will be pleasant. He will probably grill something. You don't look like a cook to me, so he will ask you to set the table. This is when you will find something, I think. You will open a drawer and find a stack of our photos. You will go into our silver cabinet and find the napkin rings finely etched with my initials.

That's when you might lose it, actually. I think it will all be too much. You will say something idiotic. Perhaps *I can't do this anymore* (as if you are actually doing something at all) or *She's killing me* (I won't even touch that one). He will do his best to look concerned, but you will realize that he's really not. He's just waiting for you to calm down, to get reasonable. You will be young—he will not choose someone who has been married before—so you will not know yet to just go upstairs to sleep. You will see his tired gaze as patronizing, which will piss you off even more. You will throw things—my crystal glasses, my plates, my jars of jam. Maybe you will even burn something. Maybe you will cut something to prove who you are and what you can do. But he is stronger than you. He will wait until you have broken as much as you can. He will wait for you to exhaust yourself. He will win.

After the fight, you will clean up in silence. If you are feisty, you will bang things around a bit more. You might go smoke a cigarette on the back porch. He will come and get you eventually. He will rub a silent hand on your back. He'll pull you inside. You'll walk together up the steps, one by one, to who knows what's ahead. I can't tell. I can see only so much. Except this. This I can see: your white palm running up the railing that is worn from my fingers. And there, in the middle of the landing, you will stop. You will gasp. And what will you both discover? Nothing. Just a splinter, tiny and painful, bleeding in your lovely, living hand.

IS THIS IT

SARAH WALTERS HAD never traveled alone before. Well, she had, between stops, from here to there. College to college, aunt's house to cousin's cottage, boyfriend's apartment in New York to lover's cabin in Maine. But never in another country by herself. Certainly not in Peru, alone on a night bus. Yet here she was, rolling south on the Pan-American Highway, sitting next to some man who kept talking and talking to her in Spanish. She didn't speak Spanish. Hadn't she made that clear by saying, probably twelve times, I'm sorry, I'm sorry, but I don't speak Spanish, *señor?* It didn't matter; he kept talking to her anyway, in a polite tone, on and on, as if she could listen, completely preventing any chance of sleep.

The reason Sarah was on this bus seemed like a noble one: she was chasing a safe man. Sarah was done with unsafe men. Actually, one unsafe man in particular — a man who tricked with lies and cheated on his cancer-ridden wife. A man who called to ask Sarah to dinner three days after his wife's ashes had been scattered on the beach. This call had shaken Sarah to the core, because an unsafe man, Sarah observed, could quite literally kill you. So safety — in the form of an old friend named Rob — was worth going to Peru for. Especially when one threw in an outside shot at love.

Rob was a good friend. A good man friend, anyway. They'd met eleven years ago at college. Junior year, she'd taken a room in a six-bedroom house Rob had leased. It was a barn of a place, a shabby brown Victorian filled with roommates. Sarah couldn't remember the other people very well now; her time in the house was now just a blur of minor dramas at birthday parties and waking up still drunk next to a pizza on the floor. What Sarah recalled most clearly were the sounds she heard. Plastic flip-flops. Popping corn. And voices. Voices everywhere.

Sarah and Rob lived in rooms next to each other. They had the type of friendship not easily defined in two words or fewer. He was a guitar player who studied engineering. She was a writer who liked to lie on the floor and listen to Gram Parsons albums. They'd flirt, and take each other to social functions when there was no one else to take. They'd ask each other about their respective romantic conquests but then edit the answers and distract each other with jokes. He was the kind of friend her boyfriends didn't like. His girlfriends, who he would always let go eventually, didn't like her either. He was, in short, a special friend. Or that's what Sarah called it.

The other roommates were delighted by them. "Why don't you guys just screw and get it over with?" they'd ask, padding by Sarah's and Rob's rooms on the way to their bongs and their mountain bikes.

Sarah and Rob would laugh it off, but in truth, Sarah didn't know why they weren't sleeping together, exactly. Sarah knew she *could* sleep with Rob. She knew it when he knocked on her wall; she knew it when he'd crawl into her bed to watch Woody Allen movies. But there were things. Little things. Rob would write his name in huge letters on the milk carton in the refrigerator so no one else would drink it. Rob would purse his lips and make meticulous lists of things he owned: his CDs, his books, how many shirts he had, what color, what size. He kept them, these lists, in a special file that he updated once a week. Rob said he didn't even know why he did that. But what Sarah knew was that she didn't think she could sleep with a man who spent an hour a week counting his own shirts.

When Sarah graduated and eventually left for New York City, she took with her the belief in the following: Rob was the man she could have if she wanted. There was evidence to support this as fact. Long after he'd given up the guitar and moved on to computers, he still sent her tapes of music he thought she'd like. He called on her birthday. He was like the backup money she stored away in the stock market. He was her safety school.

Sarah Walters was not, at thirty-one, thrilled about the fact that she now needed a safety school. The month before, on a visit home, she'd heard her mother making excuses for her on the telephone.

"Alone? Yes. But she's *fantastic!*" her mother had crowed, her head cocked to hold the receiver in a pained, awkward position. "It's not her fault things haven't worked out. She's a good-looking girl. No, I'm sorry. A *great*-looking girl." Sarah had watched her mother's back as she scrubbed furiously at a stain on the countertop.

"She's just a great-looking girl with horrible luck."

Sarah had slipped quickly out of the kitchen. She never told her mother what she'd heard, but it made Sarah think about luck. She had never considered luck before. The truth was, she *had* had pretty bad luck. Relationships that had petered out to nothing. A once-promising journalism career that had turned into fabricating content for magazines she would never actually read. Lately, even sex had turned unlucky. The other night, she'd received a call from a good-looking German she'd met on the street. In the morning, she'd found herself alone and naked in a bright, cold loft, being jolted awake by a screaming German woman. The woman pelted Sarah's back with shoes. Sarah blindly grabbed some clothes and ran out.

No, Sarah thought as she remembered attempting to hail a cab wearing only a large button-down, I do not have good luck.

But then, maybe people make their own luck. No one could say she wasn't trying. She'd sat through miserable dates with nice banker men her friends had set her up with. She paid for expensive chemical peels to burn away the wrinkles that kept popping up around her eyes. The month after Bitsy's funeral, Sarah had found a gray hair. Afterward, she'd marched straight to the telephone and made an appointment with a colorist. Then she'd perched herself on the side of her bathtub and smoked seven cigarettes.

This is not a big deal, she'd told herself fiercely. It's not like I'm dead. One gray hair does not mean I should sit here, crying alone like an idiot.

(After which she cried some more.)

And then, the week after the attack of the

German wife, Rob called her at the office. He was in Peru, traveling in between contract jobs. He'd seen *Manhattan* at a movie house in Lima, he said, and then walked to a telephone center to call her mother's house to get her number.

"Come meet me, Walters," he said. "I'm sick of traveling alone."

She paused, a bit stunned. She took a slow sip of steaming tea.

"Come *on.*" The phone crackled. "What do you have to lose?"

And Sarah could only think, OK. What the hell? Let's get to it, I'm thirty-one and so is he and we both know it's time to give this thing a chance.

So Sarah said yes and hung up the phone. She wasn't in love with him, but she thought maybe she could be if she worked on it a little. Love could be constructed; look at her parents. Look at the Clintons. It could happen. And really, it was time to face some undeniable facts. She was tired of screwing around. In fact, she was pretty tired of everything. Maybe what she wanted was to just get married already, to move into a house with vinyl siding and a gas grill and plastic pinwheels on the lawn so that she could be bored into peace.

So Sarah decided to go to South America. She wasn't much of an adventurer, really. She'd heard stories about Third World countries, stories of rapes and muggings and horrible stomach bugs that ripped you apart in bathrooms with only dirt holes for toilets. But Peru sounded like a romantic place. She packed a quart of hand sanitizer and four rolls of toilet paper, and filled her suitcase with romantic clothes—pretty skirts, sandals. In the cab on the way to the airport, she smoked and wondered what she was doing. She checked her bag and headed through security, then went straight to the bar to have a whiskey sour. She watched a show playing on the bar television about a group of people who mainly seemed to lounge on one another's sofas. Sarah observed that her own life at present involved no one on her sofa at all. She *wanted* someone on her sofa. She washed down two Valium with another drink, drifted onto the plane, and slept all the way to the other hemisphere.

*   *   *

Sarah had never sucked on the fur of a dead cat, but the taste that festered in her mouth when she woke seemed to resemble such a thing. As she shuffled through customs, she squinted at her surroundings and listened to the voices around her. She saw glowing soda machines and souvenir shops selling ponchos and liquor. Overall, the airport looked a lot like a small version of JFK.

I can do this, she thought, straightening up a bit. She bought a Coke, found her bag, and walked out into the thick air of Lima.

Chaos followed. Women in bright shawls shouted at her. Tawny, chiseled men surrounded her, tugging at her jacket. She tried to understand what they were saying.

"What? *What?*" she cried, but they only screamed louder and grabbed at her bag. "Get away!" she yelled, scooting back through the sliding doors to get her bearings. She looked through the window and spotted a bright-blue taxi, robin's-egg blue—the color of a pack of her favorite brand of cigarettes. She marched out again past the beckoning locals, got into the blue taxi, and told the man to take her to Arequipa, the town that Rob had carefully spelled out for her. She had memorized the name, repeated it over and over in her head. She hadn't looked up exactly where it was, but how far could it be? The driver smiled at her and started driving, and Sarah's heart beat wildly as she imagined him taking her to his pueblo or villa, or whatever kind of housing they had in Peru, in order to rob her and tie her to a tree.

He did not tie her to a tree. Instead, he drove her around the corner to the station, and in a kindly manner found her a seat on the correct bus. Sarah felt as if her luck might just be changing. Maybe Peru was a magical place where everything would go just right. Nodding gratefully, she blindly reached into her purse and handed him a fistful of foreign bills that she later discovered amounted to two hundred twenty-three U.S. dollars. The man calmly nodded, pocketed the month's worth of Peruvian wages, and very quickly walked away.

So now she was on the bus, speeding down this highway to Arequipa, Rob's mysterious, exotic South American town. Although, from the window, Peru didn't look exotic to Sarah at all; corrugated tin shacks lined the roads, goats and children scurried along next to the highway. The ground was brown, the houses were brown. Every once in a while, the bus passed a muddy river in which women in bright shawls were washing laundry, and Sarah thanked herself for packing three weeks' worth of underwear.

A thousand towns and three naps later, the bus rolled to a stop at ten in the morning. Sarah looked, chest fluttering, out the window at a group of old faded buildings and yet another group of locals waiting to sell her wool socks. Behind them, she saw Rob.

He was standing next to the gate, hands in his pockets. He didn't see her at first, and she watched for a moment as he ran his hand through his hair. He had ironed his plaid shirt and tucked it into a stiff-looking pair of travel pants — the army-green, utilitarian kind that zipped off into shorts. He looked a little thinner and a little older now, but handsome, in a man-Sarah-wouldn't-have-considered-before-thirty kind of way. Sarah felt a jolt in her stomach that she hoped was excitement. She got off the bus.

"Sarah," Rob said, walking toward her. Sarah

smiled. Was she faking at all? Maybe. But who cared? She was smiling.

"Hello!" he said, hugging her. She buried her face into his chest. It was a good, honest chest. She laughed finally and looked up at his face. He beamed, and she felt herself turn red as she realized that he was sizing her up, much in the same way she had just done to him. She wondered how she was faring.

"All right," he said, picking up her suitcase. "Great to see you."

"You too."

"I'm glad you're here."

"Thanks." They stared at each other, then both burst into laughter, doubling over in the street.

"This is so bizarre," Sarah said.

"It is," Rob said. "Jeez. Let's take your stuff to the hotel."

Sarah smiled. She had forgotten that when Rob got nervous, he used words like "jeez" and "gosh" and whatever else you might care to pull from a fifties TV show. Actually, she had forgotten a lot of things about him. In her memory, his hair had been blondish, but now it was dark brown. She had remembered green eyes that were, in actuality, blue. She was relieved to see that his cheeks still dimpled pleasantly when he smiled, and that his wrists were still thick and brown and wrapped in muscle. She smiled, hooking her arm in his. Cheerfully, Rob steered her down the street.

"I can't believe that you came," he said.

"Me neither!" said Sarah, feeling strangely elated.

"Don't you just love it here?"

Sarah didn't say anything, though the honest answer was no, she didn't love it at all. To Sarah, Arequipa looked like a town that might have been all right once, but was then bombed with millions of tons of garbage. The pastel buildings were rubbed with soot and dirt. Wet trash littered the street. Still, she thought, gripping Rob's arm determinedly, it could be seen as romantic, couldn't it? A lost world buried under layers of filth? She sighed and leaned into Rob a little more, but then a moped backfired and he jumped, accidentally pushing her into the street, causing her flowered sandal to plunge into an ankle-deep puddle of warm, raw sewage.

"Oh, sorry," he said, reddening. "Gosh. I mean, *shit*."

"Exactly!" Sarah said, forcing a laugh. He looked at her blankly. "Don't worry about it, Rob." She dropped his arm and fumbled for her lighter.

"I'm so sorry," he said again. Sarah shook her head and lit a cigarette, smoking the rest of the way to the hotel as the feces squished between her toes.

The hotel was a strange place to Sarah. As a woman used to Marriotts and Holiday Inns, she found it awkward to ring a bell for entrance. After several minutes, the heavy iron door was finally opened by a weathered brown woman in a bandanna. She grumpily waved them in without speaking or looking at their faces.

"High security," Sarah said.

"It's great, isn't it?" Rob asked. Sarah looked around. The building did have a skeleton of loveliness to it. It seemed to have once been a villa of some kind, as the rooms were positioned around a courtyard and a fountain. Still, it was shabby. The floors were covered in linoleum and chipped tile. Many of the windows were broken. A few young backpackers leaned against the moldy fountain, playing cards and smoking. Sarah nodded at them, and Rob led her to their room, a small, windowless space with two twin beds. Sarah giggled when she saw them. She put down her bags and they stood, looking at each other shyly.

"So," Rob finally said, "want a drink?"

"Absolutely," Sarah said. "As soon as I scrape the crap off my feet." She washed and changed her shoes, then followed Rob to a cement area, scattered with plastic chairs and tables, that seemed to pass for a bar. Rob yelled something toward a dark hallway, and Bandanna Lady sullenly brought them two bottles of cold beer.

"So," Sarah finally said. She hated silences. "Here we are."

"Yup. Here we are."

"So tell me about your trip," Sarah said.

"Oh! Gosh."

Sarah winced.

"This trip has been fantastic. I've been to almost every country in South America."

"Fantastic," Sarah said.

"You've never been to South America before, right?"

"Yes."

"Yes, you have?"

"No. I mean, I've never been anywhere except the *Let's Go Europe* tour. But you know that, Rob."

"Oh," Rob said, swilling his beer. "Well, we'll change *that,* won't we?"

"Will we?" she asked. Sarah Walters was a frank woman. She'd come to South America for romance, not coy, friendly talk about travel. Rob, however, didn't seem to be ready yet. He ignored her, looking at the menu.

"You should try the pisco next," he said, "because I'm having another beer, but I'd like a sip of pisco too."

"All right," Sarah said, tossing her hair and leaning forward a bit to show Rob her breasts. Rob looked down her blouse and reddened. He swallowed his beer nervously.

"Well, at least you're not gay," Sarah said.

"What?" he asked, pretending to have missed her remark, despite the deathly quiet of the bar. "I—didn't catch that. Huh?"

As the day wore on, Sarah observed that the strange things she remembered about Rob had not died with age. Rather, they had bloomed. Rob made a handwritten list of every acceptable restaurant in town. Even though she was so hungry she would have eaten one of the fried rat–looking things women kept trying to hand her on the street, Rob insisted on reading every menu and assessing every interior for charm, despite the fact that every restaurant looked basically the same — dirty walls, and tables covered with plastic tablecloths. After a half hour of this, they went back to the second place they had inspected for a late lunch. They sat, facing each other, quietly eating their first meal together. Chicken, rice, beans.

"So, Walters," Rob said after beer number three, "how old are you now?"

"Thirty-one."

"Well done, Walters."

Sarah blinked. "What? For making it this far?"

"No — I mean, you look good, you know. For your age."

"I look good."

"I mean, not that old. All our other friends, they look old. You know? It's scary. But you look pretty good still." He raised his glass to her. "Nice job."

"OK, that's really a horrible thing to say, Rob."

"Really? I'm sorry, I meant it to be nice."

"It was crappy."

"Oh. Sorry." They sat in silence as Sarah stewed. Of course, it was hardly the worst thing that he could have said. She was glad not to look old. She glanced around at the other diners. Certainly, she was the youngest, prettiest woman in the establishment. True, the other occupants appeared to be quinoa farmers, but still. It was something. Just then, the door opened, and some backpackers walked in. Two young blondes, talking and giggling loudly.

"Ugh," Sarah said to Rob. "So annoying." He nodded and looked at the door.

"Oh," he said. "I know them."

"Robbie!" one of them shrieked.

Sarah blinked. "You know someone? In Peru?" she asked incredulously.

"Oh, sure. All the travelers know each other. We all go to the same places. You'll see."

The girls had now approached their table. Sarah saw that they wore the same zip-off pants as Rob, paired with brightly colored Polartec tops. They kissed and hugged Rob and sat breathlessly down beside Sarah, talking in a peppy chorus.

"Robbie, who's this?"

"We haven't seen you since Bolivia! Did you hit the hostel there with the pool?"

"It was so awesome! They had mopeds!"

"We're going to the Colca Canyon on the group thing. Are you on our group thing?"

"*Wait,*" the taller one said firmly, her mouth set in a line. She pointed to Sarah. "Robbie, who *is* this?"

"I'm Sarah Walters," Sarah said. "I came from New York. To sleep with Robbie."

The girls looked at her, saucer-eyed. Rob cleared his throat. Finally, one of the girls laughed.

"Oh, my God, you're *funny,*" she said. "I'm so glad to meet someone funny. Meg is funny, but we're all so sick of each other, we can't be funny anymore."

Having effectively neutralized Sarah, the girls resumed talking. They were taking a year off after school to travel. They were blowing all their graduation money, but whatever, it was so cheap here, they told her, they might just stay forever.

Sarah, who was not a shy woman, suddenly felt mute, unable to add anything that could possibly be interesting. Meg and Beth had been all over. They could classify entire countries by the pastries they'd eaten there or the beer they'd had. Argentina was a place with fantastic bakeries. In Bolivia, the locals were mean, but there was a prison tour you could take. Brazil was crazy, just crazy. The jury was still out on Peru, of course, but they hoped that Machu Picchu would be as awesome as everyone said. And if not, there was good river rafting, and everyone seemed to like the pisco sours.

Rob excused himself to go to the toilet. The one named Meg turned to Sarah and bummed a cigarette.

"Aren't we rude?" she said. "We haven't even asked you about your trip."

"I just got here," Sarah said. She did not like Meg or Beth. She did not like their rosy cheeks or the fact that she'd been nine and lip-synching Blondie songs by the time they were born.

"Well, we think Robbie's the best. I guess you're his girlfriend, then? He never mentioned you, but it does make sense, doesn't it? We never saw him hook up with anyone or anything, even though he's so hot."

"Never," the other agreed.

"Well, that's comforting," Sarah said, although she had to admit, the thought of Rob running around with college girls did make him more attractive in a perverse sort of way.

When Rob came back, he announced that they should all go to the museum, but the girls, presumably put off by Sarah's sourness, begged off.

"It's too expensive, Robbie," Meg said, leaning into him in a way Sarah despised. "We need to save our money for the club later. But we'll see you there, though, right?"

"Goodbye," Sarah said to them pointedly, and they left, twittering.

"Funny girls," Rob said. He stood and put his hand out. "Anyway. Want to go?"

That night, Rob and Sarah tried sex. It was a clumsy effort that came about after forcing down about five pisco sours apiece. Sarah tried all the tricks. She pulled off her shirt and lingered by the window. She walked to him slowly, and then pressed his head in a tender manner to her breasts. She tried to take herself out of the ugly, cheap hotel room and put herself in an exotic movie. After all, she was in Peru. This was movie material. What would Ingrid Bergman do when making love to Rick in Morocco? How about Ava Gardner in Mexico? She arched her back, tossed her hair behind her, tilted her head toward the sky.

When he reached up to kiss her, though, the acting was over. Sarah knew well the difficulties involved in feigning passion with a bad kisser; the fact that the bad kisser was an old friend brought the whole sham down. She let him continue, let him run his hands up and down her belly and hips, but he was just horrible at it. He was too fast, too hurried. He yanked off the rest of her clothes. He entered her clinically and pumped her fast.

"Ow!" she finally said when Rob grabbed her hips suddenly and forced them upward.

"Oh, sorry, Walters," he said. "Um—ohhh." He collapsed on top of her with a groan. Sarah pushed him gently to the side.

"OK," he said. "Wow."

Sarah Walters kissed him. Was this her life now? Was she really going to settle for this? Just then, Rob put his arm around her.

"Good night, sweetheart," he said fondly, and, surprising herself, Sarah closed her eyes and felt almost happy. Sarah Walters had learned enough not to ask questions when she was almost happy. She knew that where this sort of thing was concerned, it was usually best to just shut the hell up and work with what she had.

The next morning, Rob announced that they would be heading to Cuzco.

"Who?" Sarah asked.

"Walters, didn't you read anything before you got here? It's the Incan capital."

"Great." Sarah was not feeling very conversational. She was hung over, and had just discovered that Peruvians served coffee in a form of syrup that smelled not unlike turpentine.

"It's where we start our trek to Machu Picchu."

Sarah nodded quietly.

"You do know about Machu Picchu, don't you?"

"Yes. The Megs filled me in on it. The awesome place where they sacrificed the virgins."

"So, you want to go, then?"

"Sure. Although right now what I want is a latte," she said. "I'm dying here."

The flight to Cuzco was short and uneventful. Sarah felt an odd sense of calm as the plane's wings grazed the wisps of icy snow cloud trailing off the summits of the Andes. Rob, his arm hooked in Sarah's, read a history book while she looked out the window.

Cuzco was prettier than Arequipa. Sarah brightened as she took in the polished stone houses and large town squares.

"It looks kind of like Spain," she said to Rob, feeling worldly.

"Yeah, well, it used to look *Incan* until the Spanish leveled everything," Rob said.

The hostel Rob picked was dirtier than the one in Arequipa. As she changed into some red capri pants, she could hear shrieking from the bar below.

"God," she said. "American travelers are rowdy, aren't they?"

Rob smiled and kissed her. He hesitated, then pulled her down on the bed. "Not as rowdy as we're going to be later," he whispered. Sarah laughed. She hadn't wanted to, but she couldn't help it. Rob reddened and sat up.

"I'm sorry," she said. "It's just, I'm not used to you like this."

"It's fine," he said.

"Come back."

"Not right now." He dug through her purse and lit a cigarette. "Damn it. How do you smoke these stupid things?" He took another drag and opened a shuttered window.

Just then, a familiar voice pierced the air in the courtyard.

"Robbie! Robbie, we *know* you're in here!"

"I thought they were on the group thing," Sarah said. Rob didn't answer. He leaned over the balcony.

"Hey, Meg."

"Robbie, we skipped Colca. We met these Dutch guys with a car and just hitched to Cuzco. How awesome is that?"

"Pretty awesome," Rob said.

A few seconds later they barged into the room. They had zipped off the pant bottoms this time, revealing strong, tan legs. Meg took off her jacket and was left wearing only a sports bra. Sarah watched Rob look at her, then quickly look away.

"Anyway, we're going down to the square to check things out. Do you two want to come?"

Rob smiled and nodded, then remembered Sarah.

"Um, what do you think? Do we?"

"You go ahead, Robbie," Sarah said.

Rob ignored the dig. "We'll be back," he said, and they left.

Sarah took off her skirt and sweater, bathed as best she could, and lay down on the bed, naked.

She slept for a while, then woke up confused and disoriented, looking at the ceiling fan, wondering what she was doing, why she was there. She thought about going out, but then, why bother, when she could enjoy a Peruvian sandwich in her room and watch Peruvian TV from her bed? Suddenly, Sarah didn't understand the point of traveling at all. She felt limp, like a piece of lint, moving from spot to spot, seeing things she could just as easily look at in the encyclopedia she had at home. There must be some way of establishing permanence, she thought. Of leaving your mark on a place.

She got up and dressed, then lined up her shirts and socks in the drawer. She put her toiletries out on the glass shelf. She ate nothing, because her body felt out of tune; she had vomited twice so far. She curled up in a ball, stared at the wall, and waited for Rob to come back.

Four hours later, he returned, drunk, with the Megs.

"You should have come and found us," he said, as they fell, laughing, onto his bed.

"Sorry, I haven't had the tracking chip installed quite yet."

"Ohhhhhhh," Meg said, raising her tan fingers to her perfect lips. "Let's go."

"Dognap!" Rob shrieked nonsensically, at which the three of them dissolved into laughter again. Rob looked at Sarah. "Sorry, sorry — private joke."

Sarah lay back down, and the Megs finally left. Rob lay down beside her.

"You OK?" he asked. Sarah nodded, still irritated as Rob clumsily fumbled at her skirt and underwear. Drunkenly, he climbed on top of her. She closed her eyes for a while, and then finally looked up. What she saw surprised her. Not only were his eyes closed but they were screwed shut with determination, as if he were trying, very hard, to hide from something.

At that moment, Sarah Walters realized that she wasn't the only one pretending to herself that this was where she wanted to be.

"Rob?"

He opened his eyes slowly, and stopped. He fell away from her.

"Walters." He wiped his forehead, and she saw that he was already limp. Sarah pressed her face into the pillow.

"Oh, Walters," he said, patting her shoulder. "It was a good try."

"*I'm sick of trying*," Sarah said, her voice muffled by the scratchy pillowcase.

"Oh, Walters. It's not you, you know. I love you."

Sarah rolled over and snorted.

"Really, I do." Rob patted her arm again. "And, I mean, I don't have to. No one *has* to love you. I just think that maybe... well, you've gotten so..."

He paused, carefully.

"I just think we missed our window."

So there it was. In Cuzco, on a musty, thin mattress, the truth came out. Sarah Walters had come to Peru to chase Rob because he was the only one who had always wanted her. He was her sure thing. And then, guess what? He didn't want her after all. It was almost funny. No, it *was* funny, Sarah decided. *Ha,* she thought.

Ha.

In the morning, Sarah woke early and went down to breakfast. She found that she was incredibly hungry and ordered a breakfast called the *Americano,* which turned out to be a plate of eggs. She wondered if it was OK to eat eggs from a Peruvian chicken. She wondered if Peruvian chickens understood Spanish. She wondered if chickens understood anything at all. She ate her eggs.

Rob came and joined her.

"How are you?"

"Fine."

Rob ordered something in Spanish and stirred his coffee.

"Walters, I—"

"Forget it."

"Have you made plans?"

"What do you mean?" Sarah had not made plans. She had planned that Rob would take her back to the airplane.

"Well, to get to Lima."

"I have no idea how to get to Lima."

"Well, I…"

"You need to take me to Lima, Rob. You got my ass down here, now take me back."

"The thing is, I'm going to Machu Picchu with Meg and them. So…you know."

"Oh," she said. "Right." She took a last sip of coffee. "I guess I do."

So Sarah Walters finished her breakfast and told herself that this was her own decision. She left the hostel café, with its crumbling stucco walls and ugly, folksy furniture. She went to the tiny, dark room she and Rob had shared so unsuccessfully, packed her suitcase, and came back to the table to announce that she was leaving that night.

Rob walked her to the bus station. She would be going to Lima via Ica, an oasis, the Peruvian version of a resort town. There were sand dunes there, the guidebook said. And a lagoon. She would spend the night there. Do the travel-alone thing. Have some fun.

"You'll have a great time," Rob said.

"Absolutely, Rob. What girl wouldn't want to travel six thousand miles to stare at a huge pile of South American sand?"

"*Peruvian* sand," Rob said. "Swimming pools. Cocktails." He looked around. "Free love."

"That's what I came for, isn't it?" Once again, he ignored her. She stood in front of the bus while Rob took her picture. He kissed her cheek, handed her suitcase to the driver, and walked away. She watched through the window as he bought a chocolate bar from a woman with thick, glossy braids. Then he left the bus station without looking back.

Sarah settled into the seat. Ica is about five hundred miles away from Cuzco. Before there were highways and buses and cars, it took Peruvian pilgrims entire seasons to travel from one great capital to the other. Even now, one must weave down mountain highways, passing through tiny village towns. One must cross the Apurímac River and brush the Andes Mountains. The entire trip was to take Sarah Walters roughly fifteen hours. As the bus gasped and started, she realized that she had no magazine, no drugs, no English-speaking person with which to pass the time.

Sarah spent the first few hours staring out the window, but after the second time she'd vomited into a bread bag provided by the worried old woman beside her, she simply shut her eyes, breathing in and out, wishing for sleep. It wasn't fair that she couldn't sleep. It wasn't fair that she had spent a fifth of her savings account on this trip. It wasn't fair that Rob hadn't loved her, that she hadn't loved Rob, that she was too numb to fall in love at all anymore.

Oh, shut up, she thought. She was so sick of herself. No wonder Rob had passed on her. She opened her eyes and looked out again, but the anger remained. Nothing—none of it—was fair. Even this goat herder standing next to the road had more satisfaction in his life than Sarah did. She'd gladly trade with him. *Here,* she imagined saying, *let's just trade. Here's a plane ticket,* señor. *Welcome to my useless life.*

What Sarah Walters did not know was that, oblivious to what might be fair or love, a small goat had just strayed away from the herder. Through the roar of the bus, Sarah Walters could not have heard the goat herder call to the missing animal, could not have realized that the shaggy thing, upon hearing the herder's voice, shot out onto the road. The driver yelled and swerved, and for one brief instant, the bus tilted up onto two wheels. Screams erupted, and Sarah Walters felt herself float up, heard the woman beside her cry out, saw the old goat herder's brown-and-yellow eyes widen in terror as she hovered above him like a lover.

*   *   *

Fear does different things to different people. In Sarah's case, it sparked a strange series of synaptic firings in her mind as it began to flit, frantically, from one truth to another. She loved Rob. She didn't love Rob. She loved tea—mint tea, not from a tea bag but brewed in a pot. That actor in *Stealing Home* was the same guy in *Ghostbusters*. She was pregnant. She was twenty-six. No. She was thirty-one. She didn't want to die today, in this red-clay country. She liked to swim in blood-warm summer water. Rivers and lakes meshed with marsh. She was going to have a—

Jesus Christ. What? Christ.

She was going to have a baby. Of course she was. She had never been late, or nauseated, in her entire life. *It's Rob.* No, that didn't work, did it? *It's Meg.* Meg? *It was the German.* It was the German. With the loft and the wife and the shoes. It was the German who, of course, would never, ever know.

So.

The bus righted itself with little incident. The driver swore at the goat herder, but other than that, it was over. The grandmother next to her put her hand on Sarah's shoulder.

"Mother," Sarah told her, wrapping her arms around her newly precious self. "I'm going to be a mother."

The woman smiled and handed her another bag, obviously assuming she was going to be sick again. Sarah took it. The woman stroked her hair, and talked and talked. She talked to Sarah over the mountains, through the vast desert, along the coast as the sea rushed by. Sarah sat back and listened to the words. She wondered what the woman was saying to her. Maybe they were horrible, disgusting things. Or maybe they were the sweetest, kindest things Sarah Walters would never understand in her life.

GRASS

IT HAPPENS WHEN his wife is next to
the sushi table.

My daughter is over on a picnic blanket,
screaming at some kid over a plastic horse. We're
back home for a visit, just a short trip down from
New York, and my old friend Annie happened
to be having a party. I'm standing in her yard
awkwardly, drinking wine out of a limp plastic
cup.

My friend Bitsy's family used to live here.
Bitsy died two years ago in an unladylike manner involving chemo, whiskey, and an unadvised
number of pain pills. When she was here, it was
a respectable Southern house filled with antique

furniture and paintings of dead relatives. Now everything is modern Pottery Barn and cream, but the yard is the same, a sheet of green grass rolling thick down to South Battery. I've kicked off my flip-flops and am standing there barefoot. It feels like youth under my feet.

Lee and I haven't really talked in years, probably since I said goodbye to him at my mother's insistence. That day I climbed into my bed and sobbed for days, sniffling into a handful of crumpled toilet paper, pushing my face into my stained pillow in despair. I thought he'd come back, but boys like Lee don't need to be told to go twice. I don't remember what I did after that, probably went to a mosquito-infested party in the woods with Charlotte, drank beer, smoked cigarettes. And even though I distinctly remember telling myself I'd never get over it, the dull, sickening pain of the broken heart, I did, with the help of other boys, tall boys in New England sweaters and faded baseball caps. Of course, truthfully, I guess that would mean that I didn't ever really get over anything. I just forgot about Lee. His face was painted over by others until he became nothing more than a story.

A package carefully wrapped in blue tissue and tucked away in the back of my mind.

I don't know why Lee is at this party. Maybe he's friends with Annie's husband. Who knows. We've run into each other a few times, and at first I would try to start some witty banter. Something light to show him that I'm over it, we can laugh now, it's been years and we're old and can't we just be funny about it, for God's sake? But he was always pretty miserable at conversation, and it became one of those efforts that's so hard you don't bother, like changing your own oil when you can pay the gas-station guy to do it for you in ten minutes or less.

But now we are on the lawn. I am so out of it, it took me a moment to realize that Annie's new fancy house is really Bitsy's former elegantly shabby one. In fact, I probably wouldn't have put it together for hours if Lee hadn't been standing there on the grass, in the same spot where he stood all those years before, smiling at me in his nineteen-year-old body, skinny and golden, with his hands in his pockets. He's less skinny now, and the blond is gone from his hair, but he's still recognizable, a good-looking man who used to be godlike once. It's one of those ridiculous moments when you are slapped in the face with such a déjà vu that you feel like a walking cliché. But that's where clichés come from, I guess. They happen.

He introduces me to his pretty wife. He is a real-estate developer now, he says. He sold the farm years ago. His wife's job is something impressive, but I don't really hear. A lawyer, maybe. Or a decorator. Jessie is hanging on to my jeans, and she tumbles away to play some game they've set up for her. The pretty wife goes to the sushi table, and we are left standing there, Lee and I, on Bitsy's grass, looking at each other.

Right then, I feel everything peel away. All the other times I've been kissed, the lines on my face and body, the fact that I have been split and stretched to let another person out into the afternoon sun. He doesn't bother to talk, and I don't either, but we look. We stare. And for a moment, I am sure of everything. For a second, with my bare feet on the fresh thick grass, there has not been, for any of us, even one mistake.

DREAMING IN COLOR

I DON'T DREAM like I used to. I used to close my eyes at night and wake up to blinding visions. I'd spend my mornings dazed, dizzy with memories of snowy skin and blue grass and effervescent light. Now I just open my eyes and look at the ceiling. I'm not sure when that changed.

My daughter, Jessie, and I are driving in my dead father's truck. I have always wanted my own truck, and now I've got it, a real Ford beauty, wheels as high as my hips and a plastic-lined bed that can hold one hundred gallons of anything. Bread. Milk. Diamond rings. There is nothing back there now, but it feels good to

have that space, just in case we need to cart ourselves somewhere and hole up for good.

"Where are we going?" my little girl says.

"Somewhere special," I say back. For her, I
try to make everything special. The supermar-
ket. The funeral home. "Look," I say, holding
up a cut-glass doorknob at the hardware store,
"treasure."

"Let's keep it," Jessie says. She just turned
four, and she understands things. "Let's buy it
and keep it and put it away."

We have been home for three weeks since
my father's funeral. By home, I mean my mother's house outside Charleston. It's not really
my home anymore. My sister and I have agreed
that my mother should probably sell it and buy
something smaller in town. But progress is slow.
I showed her a carpeted condo where some of
my friends' mothers live, but she told me she
doesn't want to live with the other widows.
She said that she doesn't want company while
she waits to die. She hates that she's getting old,
and I hate that she hates it, so we spend most
of our time being overly polite and playing with
my daughter.

"Pretty girl," she is saying, brushing Jessie's blond hair. "Pretty pretty pretty girl."

"She is pretty, isn't she?" I say.

"So pretty," my mother says.

"Mom," I say, "listen. We should really talk about the house. I've got a list of realtors."

"So pretty." She reaches over and picks my daughter up. Jessie does not like to be picked up. She usually screams and slaps your hand away. Since my dad's funeral, though, she's started to let my mother hold her. My daughter, she's already kinder than me.

The phone calls are dwindling. At first, the house was full of women. As lifetime members of the Camellia Society, my mother and I can be assured of a certain amount of social interaction. This is because the three main purposes of the Society are to teach children to ballroom dance, prepare women for proper marriage, and ensure that no Camellia faces death alone. As a result of our sisterhood, women in flowered dresses have brought potato casserole and vats of ham and macaroni pie. I've gained seven pounds. The food's not for me, though. It's for my mother, and she's not eating any of it. She's growing thinner every day. The women — Mrs. Ravenel, Mrs. Mitchell, Mrs. Jones-Simmons, Mrs. Legare, among others — came for lunch several days in a row. They drank pink wine on the porch and talked about anything but my father. My mother did well. She put on nice clothes and had her hair done and pretended, in the proper Camellia manner, that it was a party. Then came the seventh afternoon, exactly a week after my father had put a pistol in his mouth and pulled the trigger. That day she sobbed and threw a crystal glass at Mrs. Mitchell and screamed like a prisoner of war. The women all kissed her and left except for Georgia, our Camellia-turned-lesbian. Georgia force-fed my mother whiskey and pills and rocked her back and forth in her arms until she passed out.

Things have calmed since then. My sister had to go back to Washington; she's an environmental lobbyist and has the world to save. I called my editor at the magazine and took a leave. He understood, saying that he'd find a freelancer to cover my beat: the latest beauty developments for today's tweens. Just speaking to him over my father's telephone made me feel like a whore. I promised I'd check in, but so far I haven't.

My old friend Charlotte calls. We haven't talked in a couple of years, but hearing her voice feels like the sun through fog.

"I'm so sorry for your loss," she says formally. "How long are you staying?"

"I don't know," I say. "Mom's in pretty bad shape. Jessie and I are living with her in my old room."

"God. That sucks," she says, as if picturing the reality of my situation has jolted her into honesty. "How are you?"

"Good. My new ready-to-wear line's doing really well. I'm opening a store in LA. Blah blah fucking blah. The usual."

"I see your stuff in magazines all the time. The ads and all."

"Yeah, it's all pretty great. I'll send you some samples. You're a six, right?"

"Eight. Maybe a ten right now."

"No problem. I'll send you some jersey pieces."

"Great," I say.

"You know," she says, "everything's going

to work out for you, Sarah. Honestly. I know it seems like it won't, but someday, this will all pass, and you'll get everything—"

"I wish for," I say. I step out onto the porch and light a cigarette.

"Yeah."

"I remember."

"It's true."

"But you know what, Char?" I say. "You've been saying that for years. Ever since I've known you. You said that you'd be famous, and I'd get everything that I wished for. And when you said it, when we were, like, sixteen or whatever, I believed you. But I thought you meant soon. I didn't think you meant that at thirty-five I'd still be sitting around waiting for it to happen."

"Well," Charlotte says, "I *am* famous."

"That's true," I say, laughing a little. She laughs too.

"So what the hell'd you wish for, anyway?" she asks.

I look at the water, thinking. "You got me, lady," I say finally. "I have no idea."

*　　*　　*

The Camellias stopped visiting in person after Mom's fit, but she is acting fairly normal, so every couple of days I leave my daughter with her and drive the truck around alone. My father did not leave it to me specifically, but my mother refuses to be seen in a truck, so I guess it's up to me to either drive it or sell it for the cash. She's been missing out. It feels so good to drive a truck, high off the road, dust and rocks flying up, dinging against the undercarriage. Today I pointlessly drive for half an hour, just looking around, then feel guilty because I've been wasting time when we have nothing for dinner. I finally threw out the spoiling Camellia food yesterday, and now that there's no man to cook for, my mother has nothing in her refrigerator except for American cheese and tomatoes from her garden. I stop at the barbecue stand and get some pulled pork and boiled corn and fried hush puppies, Jessie's new favorite.

"Sarah." I turn around. It's J.T., a boy Charlotte used to date when we were in high school. Except he's not high school age anymore, he's thickened with the years, just like me.

"Hey, J.T." I do the once-over. J.T. is old-school. He is wearing a camouflage shirt, and his neck and arms are the color of freshly boiled crab. He has a truck too. From his outfit, I'm guessing it's filled with dead ducks.

"You look nice," he says.

"Thank you."

"Sorry about your dad. Unexpected."

"Yeah, well." There is a silence that, surprisingly, is not awkward at all. The barbecue man brings me my food.

"You in town for long?" he asks.

"I don't know."

"Maybe I'll come around and visit."

I pause. "I've got a daughter."

"I've got a boat," J.T. says without blinking. "I'll come by."

I get back and find my mother in the porch swing with Jessie. She is brushing Jessie's hair and filling it with ribbons and talking about daddies. My mother wants things for me.

"Hey," I say.

"Howdy."

"I got us barbecue."

My daughter raises her hands and squeals. My
mother claps her hands and squeals with her. As
she does every night, my mother pulls out the
good plates and the monogrammed silver. We
eat po'boys on bone china, drink sweet tea from
crystal glasses.

"This is how you sit in your chair," she tells
Jessie. "Watch. See? Up straight. Shoulders back.
This is how you hold your fork. Elbows down.
Left hand in your lap."

After dinner, she goes upstairs and puts
makeup on my daughter while I go through a
stack of bills. My mother does not believe that
it is ladylike to do bills. She owes $12,345 to Visa
and Sears. I go look for her in the bedroom,
where she and my daughter are sitting in front
of the mirror.

"Mom," I say, "do you have your own bank
account?"

"I don't know," she says disinterestedly.
"Your father did that. You know, we should go
downtown and buy Jessie some dresses tomorrow. Maybe something for church."

I shake my head and go to my dad's desk.
I have been avoiding it. I do not want to go

through a dead man's things. My father, though, must have expected me. He left everything on his desk in neat, labeled stacks: IRA; MORTGAGE; ELOISE'S TRUST; SARAH'S TRUST. I half expect to find a note, but my father wasn't really sentimental that way. There is plenty of money, which I have to say I'm happy about. The only thing I find that's unexpected is a half-empty flask of whiskey, hidden under a Peterson bird guide. I guess it's the half-empty part that makes me weep.

Late the next morning, Georgia's car rumbles up the drive.

"Helloooo?" she calls. I come downstairs. She's wearing jeans, a T-shirt, and boots. Her hair is in braids. At what I calculate to be sixty-two, she is still, in a completely careless and undeniable way, gorgeous.

"I came to take Lady Liza to the beach."

"That sounds nice. Does she know?"

"She will in a minute." She sizes me up. "You look like hell."

"Wanna smoke?" I ask.

"Sure." We step out onto the porch and light up. I don't trust Georgia. For one, she is in love with my mother. For two, she always thought my father was an idiot. She backed off eventually. Still, I can't imagine that she's not a teeny, tiny bit happy about my father's departure, as unnecessarily violent as it was.

"Sarah Walters."

"What?"

"Stop sulking."

"Jesus, Georgia," I say, exasperated. "I'm not sulking. I'm in mourning."

"You weren't even friends with your dad. You hadn't spent time with Henry in years."

This was true. My father and I were never close. It was something I always meant to get to. But.

"Thanks for pointing that out, Georgia. It doesn't mean I don't miss him."

"Your mama misses him."

"Yeah."

"Why don't you move back here, Sarah?" Georgia says, sitting on the railing. "You could start something up here. A writing gig at the paper."

"What, the Newsless Courier?"

"Your mama needs you. You can't raise Jessie in New York."

"Don't tell me what I can and can't do, Georgia," I say. "It's not like you're such a prime example of family values."

"Yikes." Georgia flips her cigarette off the porch. "Someone's got a little chip."

"Maybe."

"There's all kinds of family," Georgia says, leveling me flat with her dark eyes. "Hey, now. I think I hear your mama."

Mom comes out onto the porch, eyes squinted at the sun. She must have taken a sedative on top of the gin last night.

"Hey, George."

"Came to take you to the beach."

"No, thank you." My mother collapses onto the patio sofa.

"You don't want to go to the beach?"

"No, Georgia. Stop talking to me like I'm twelve."

"All right, I'll try again. Hey, Liza, I think it's time for you to get your scrawny ass out of this house."

"I don't want to go to the fucking beach, Georgia." I look over. I've never heard my mother say "fucking" in her life. Georgia sits down next to her and puts her arm around her and leaves it there. I expect Mom to flick it off, but she doesn't. Instead she puts her head on Georgia's shoulder. "George, I'm just not up to it."

"Shhhhh. That's OK, Liza," Georgia says. The scene makes me queasy. I don't want it to, really I don't. But would this be happening if Dad were here?

"Can y'all keep an eye on Jessie?" I ask. "I gotta run an errand."

By the time they've said yes, I'm down the steps, headed out.

I come back to find Georgia replaced, to my surprise, by J.T.

Mom is giggling like a twelve-year-old. Jessie is staring at them both distrustfully, just like I've taught her to.

"Hey," I say. "I thought you might call first."

"People around here don't call," he says,

standing up. He is tall. He'd be handsome if
not for the crooked nose, broken in a bar fight
I still vaguely recall. "Remember? They just
come by."

"OK." I shift on my feet.

"John Thomas, would you like a cocktail?"
my mother asks. "I bet Sarah would love to
make you a gin and tonic."

" 'J.T.' is 'John Thomas'?"

"Of course," he says. "But no gin for me,
though."

"Too early?" my mother asks.

"Too good," J.T. says. "I can't have gin anymore. I like it too much."

We stare at him a bit too long, until J.T. says,
"Anyway, come on. I brought the boat."

I forgot about Southern men.

I have had plenty of men in my life. Too
many, certainly, by Camellia standards. Still, I
have had only one Southern lover. In my messy
search, I abandoned the South long back. The
men here are too old-fashioned. Too slow. Still,
there's something to be said for a man who

jumps out and opens your car door for you. A man who, even when your virtue is long dried up and scattered, will always, no matter what, call you ma'am.

J.T. has the boat docked and ready at the landing next to our house. It's just a johnboat, but it's spotless, and the lines are perfectly coiled. He's packed a cooler of seltzer and Coke for us, and has boiled peanuts in a Ziploc. Jessie tries to keep quiet, but it's pretty obvious she's about to explode with happiness. She sits up front with a huge grin on her face, skimming her hand over the warm green river, waving to the cranes and gulls that watch her nonchalantly from the rich mudflats.

I watch her carefully and steal looks at J.T. I can't decide if he's handsome or not. I like his eyes, brown like warm coffee. His sideburns are a little weird. He's got a nice smile and is big through the shoulders. He loses points for the can of dip.

"She's having a good time," J.T. says.

"It's a great little boat."

"It's good for fishing, gigging flounder, all

that. I take it hunting in the fall. You should come."

"Maybe. I don't know if we'll be here that long."

"Your mama's all alone, isn't she? You should at least stay through the fall."

"She's got friends." I cross my arms. I don't like being pressured. Jessie squeals at a dolphin. "What happened with the drinking?"

"I don't know. I was just drinking every day, and I realized it wasn't good for me. You ever do something just because it's good for you?"

"Nope," I say. "To tell you the truth, generally I do just the opposite."

"I think I know something that'd be good for you."

"What, you think I drink too much?" From the bow, Jessie turns her head around and stares at us.

"Shit, girl, I don't know if you drink too much. I was just trying to ask you to dinner tomorrow." J.T. grins.

"Oh," I say.

"So, you wanna?"

"Sure."

"Yee-haw!" He slaps his knee and guns the boat, then puts a wad of Skoal in his lower lip.

Yes. Southern men. Different.

When I ask my mother to watch Jessie, she is suspicious. "You're going on a date with John Thomas?" she asks. "Where to? What are you going to wear? What time will you be home?"

"I don't know, don't know, don't know."

"Well, I can see that you don't want me to say anything."

"You can say whatever you want."

"All I have to say is that he seems *very* nice."

"Did you think any more about the house today?"

"Too busy. Had to iron your sheets."

"That's crazy, Mom. Get the new kind that don't wrinkle. God, I'll buy you some." My mother turns away and picks up a silver hand mirror on my dresser. "Anyway, we have to figure this out soon. I mean, I know you like the house now, but after we go back to New York, you're going to be really lonely out here."

"Do you think it's strange he doesn't drink?" my mother asks. Like me, she is extremely good at ignoring any attempt at reason.

"A little."

"Is he in that club for former drinkers?"

"I don't think so. He says he stopped drinking just because being sober was better for him."

"Noble." My mother picks a blue dress out of the pile and puts it on the bed. "Although I find it hard to trust a man who doesn't drink."

"Yeah, well." I hold the blue cloth up under my chin and look in the mirror. The fact is that my dad drank plenty, and he ended up shooting himself in the next room with no warning. At present, trust is probably outside of our realm of possibility.

J.T. shows up late, which is good. He is wearing blue and khaki, and I am glad to see that he appears wrinkled, meaning he didn't go home and shower for our date. As he approaches the porch, I wonder why it is that the worse a man treats me, the better-looking he gets.

I have let my mother do my hair. She likes big

hair, so I end up looking like a cross between
Doris Day and Beaker on *The Muppet Show.* J.T.
doesn't seem to mind. He tells me that I look
nice, which I probably do by Island standards. He
clears fishing tackle off the car seat to make room
for me, and when he turns the car on, a man is
talking about God on the radio.

"Are you religious?" I ask.

"About some things," J.T. says. He doesn't
say anything else about it. But he doesn't turn
the radio off, either. He takes me to a seafood
shack, where a black man older than my dead
father shovels steaming, crusty oysters onto
tables covered in newspaper, and orders himself
a Coke and me a beer.

"Oh, I don't need beer."

"Look, I'm not going to deprive you of beer
just because I'm not drinking it."

"Thanks." I'm grateful. Oysters are salty, and
I don't know if I could deal with a date without
beer. We chat for a while about life since we last
saw each other. Me: Northern college, delusions
of grandeur, pointless magazine work, bad relationships, constant questioning, one fabulous
daughter. Him: college in town, buying a house

and fixing it up, buying four houses and fixing them up, marriage, divorce, renewed faith (he had some to begin with), two good dogs.

"So," he says carefully after I crack my second tall-boy, "how did Jessie come about?"

"Come about?"

"You know. You haven't mentioned her dad yet. Where'd that pretty little girl come from?"

It annoys me that he's asking this. It annoys me even more that I am taken in by the fact that he called Jessie pretty.

"I got drunk and screwed someone." As soon as it comes out of my mouth, I regret it. "Sorry."

He waits a moment.

"Sore subject?"

"Not at all. Jessie's the best thing that ever—I mean, that sounds stupid, but honestly, she's been this awesome phenomenon for me. My life was completely out of order before I had her, and then, suddenly, I had this purpose. It's just that the father part sounds so bad. There's no good way to tell it. The fact is that I don't talk to him. I know who he is, but he has a wife and stuff, and I didn't want to bother him. And also, I wanted... I just wanted..."

"You wanted her all to yourself?"

"Yes! Shit, I've never told anyone that, but it's kind of true. I didn't want to share her, and certainly not with someone we didn't know or love."

J.T. is quiet for a minute, which I take to mean that he thinks I am disgusting. I drink some more of my beer.

"So you never tried to contact the father."

I look him straight in the eye. "No."

I let the word ring for a second, and it does—a big, fat gong.

J.T. nods and sucks down an oyster. "I think you did the right thing."

"You do?"

"Why expose her to a father who doesn't want her?"

"Yes. *Yes.* Exactly. No one else gets that."

J.T. nods again. "Probably not," he says. "But I think people do different things for different reasons. It seems to me that if those reasons are honest, then they are good and right. You sound pretty honest to me."

"About this," I say carefully, "I am very honest."

"She's pretty great."

"Isn't she?" I open another oyster. They are beautiful things, oysters. I've been eating them since I had teeth. Where steamed oysters are concerned, you want to find a large one with a tight seal. Not too tight; too tight means it's either old or spoiled. I find it a good sign that J.T. has brought me to this oyster shack. It says he knows things about me. He knows that to a girl raised on the marsh, there is something about finding the perfect oyster that spells hope.

J.T. does not kiss me good night. He walks me to the door, leans against it, and looks me up and down, from the top of my head to my shoes. It's hotter than a kiss. I turn red, a phenomenon so lost to me that I bring my hand to my face, thinking something is wrong.

"That was fun," he says.

"Yes. It was a nice night."

"Would you like to go out again?"

"Sure."

"My church... our church —"

"Ah, J.T.? I don't do church."

"Your mama still does church."

"Do you..."—it sounds so ridiculous—"do church?"

"I listen," he says. "I'm trying to figure it out."

I cut to the chase. "If you try to born-again me, I'll be out of here so fast—"

"What, like you've got it all figured out?"

"I'm not doing church."

"OK. How about the church fish fry?"

"Oh, right. The fish fry." The last time I went to the fish fry, I was sixteen. I drank too much beer and lost my virginity to a farmer.

"I know, it's square, but maybe Jessie could come. And your mama could get out of the house. They have rides and ponies and all. Could be fun, or at least funny."

"OK, let's, um..." J.T. grabs my hand and kisses it. He plays with a curl on my shoulder.

"I'll pick you all up on Sunday at three," he says, answering my hesitation. He looks at me like I'm someone special, gets in his car, and drives away.

My mother is still awake and sitting on the screened-in porch upstairs. She has, no doubt, been listening to every word. I go out and join her.

"How was your evening?" she asks.

"Fine."

"You going out again?"

"I don't know. Maybe." I sit near her in a wicker chair. I hate wicker. It bites. Why does everyone in the South insist on wicker?

"Sounds to me like you'll see him again."

"Mom. Stop." I really want to smoke, but even at thirty-five, I can't manage to pull out a cigarette in front of my mother. "Why are you sitting in the dark?" I ask.

"The bulb's out."

"So?"

My mother swirls the ice in her before-bed gin. "You need a ladder to change that bulb."

"So?"

"I don't know where it is."

It takes me a moment to process this information. "You don't know where the ladder is?"

My mother doesn't answer.

"It's probably in the garage, right?"

"It doesn't matter. I'll call Georgia to help me with it tomorrow."

"Mom, it's a lightbulb. I can change it. I'll just stand on a chair."

"No!" I look over, surprised. My mother's mouth is set into a frown. "The way to do it is with the ladder."

"All right. So I'll find the ladder."

"Do you think that John Thomas could do it?"

"Come on, Mom," I say cheerfully, standing up with purpose. "You've got to get used to being alone. Let's change that bulb. I'll show you how."

It's not a bad idea. It comes from the right place. I can take charge, I think. I will lead a cheerful crusade and my mother will become self-sufficient and plucky, a regular steel magnolia. But this is one of the reasons why I'm stupid. Because what my mother does is give me a withering look. She gets up silently and brushes past me.

"I will never," she says icily, "do anything to get used to being alone." I hear her pour some more gin from the decanter she keeps in her room before she closes the door.

*   *   *

It is decided that we will all go to the church fish fry—myself, Jessie, Mom, and Georgia, who has become a semipermanent fixture in the house.

"Is it OK?" I ask J.T. over the phone.

"Of course."

"But, I mean, now you're towing this gaggle of women."

"Gaggles are OK," he says.

"You're really very nice."

"Probably not as nice as you think."

I am glad to hear him say it.

"There's one more thing. Mom won't ride in a truck."

"Interesting."

"So we'll have to go in her car or Georgia's."

"We'll take two cars, then," he says. "Truck's nonnegotiable."

"OK," I say. "You're in for it."

Aside from the funeral, this is Mom's first official outing since Dad died, and she dresses appropriately, Camellia-style. She puts Jessie in a pink dress and curls her hair, and I fish a skirt out of my bag and iron it. Even Georgia showers, brushes her hair, and puts on loafers. Truly, this is an occasion.

"Do you think he'll be on time?" Mom asks. "Always a good sign when a man's on time."

"I used to like them to come as late as possible, myself," Georgia says.

"God, Georgia," Mom says. "Well, I like John Thomas a lot."

"Thanks, Mom."

"Even if he doesn't drink."

"The man doesn't drink?" Georgia says. "Dear God."

"Shut up, Georgia, OK?"

"Shut up. Shut up." Jessie is in a phase where she latches on to words. It's an irritating new habit she has developed in the last three months.

"Jessie—"

"Sarah, don't tell Georgia to shut up."

"Jesus."

"Jesus. Jesus. Jeeeeesus."

"Jessie, stop! My God, we're going to drive each other insane."

"You think," Georgia says, "there's anything about this house that's not insane?"

"I don't know," I answer. "But you're not helping."

The doorbell rings.

"Insane," Jessie chirps. "Insane."

Our caravan is a slow one. Jessie and I ride with J.T., while Georgia drives Mom in the sedan behind us. The church is twenty minutes away, but J.T. drives slowly, careful not to lose the other car.

"J.T.," I say, annoyed, "they know how to get there."

"I'm just being polite," he says.

Still, I am irritated. I can't figure out why. I am irritated at his niceness and at my skirt and at his clean khakis. I'm irritated that I'm irritated. Damn.

We arrive, our awkward flock, and make our way toward the food. I've forgotten that they fry fish whole here. Head on, eyes bulging, the works.

All of the awkwardness that hadn't yet plagued J.T. and me is between us now. We stand together stiffly. There are people here that I haven't seen since I was sixteen. They all nod in sympathy and pay their respects to my mother. Georgia sticks to her like an old refrigerator magnet.

I see my old friend Annie administering the desserts, in the manner of the good Charleston wife she now is. I tell J.T. I'll be right back, then move away with relief.

"Annie."

"Sarah! Hi!" Annie's cheeks are flushed. She is busy serving cake, cookies, and pies that she obviously made herself to feed the only-slightly-grateful masses. She has always been too nice.

"Anne, take over, 'kay?" Annie says to her daughter as she hands her tiny doppelgänger the cake knife.

"She looks just like you."

"I know." Annie rolls her eyes. "Big-boned."

"Pretty."

"Thanks, sweetie. So how are you holding up?"

"I'm OK."

"I see Georgia's here," Annie says, frowning.

"Yup. She's been a good friend, actually."

"Sarah"—Annie looks around—"I need to make sure you know something. What people are saying, I mean."

"Annie, it's been a long time since I gave a rat's ass about what people in Charleston say."

"I know. You and your friend Charlotte never did. But just in case, OK? It's about Georgia."

"What about her? She's gay? God forbid."

Annie takes a deep breath. "People are saying your mom and Georgia are having an affair."

I am surprised, but feign indifference. "God, Annie, who cares if they are? Let the old girls have their fun, then."

"You don't understand." Annie puts her hand on my arm to try to make me focus on what she is saying. "Georgia was living at your house for months."

"What?"

"Before your father killed himself. It's true. I went myself to bring by a pie. People were talking and I...I was concerned."

"Or maybe you just wanted to get a look for yourself?"

"I'd never do that, Sarah. I *swear.* But she was there, Georgia, I mean, sitting with your mother...intimately. I don't know. It doesn't matter. But people are saying—"

"I get it, Annie," I say. "I can guess what they're saying."

I look over at J.T. He's talking to a guy with a beer belly. These fucking fish fries.

"I'm sorry, Sarah. I just thought you should know."

"It's OK, Annie." I kiss her cheek. "I gotta go now, OK?"

"Hey, guess what? Little Anne is starting Cotillion Training School next week," Annie says. "She's going to be a Camellia. Isn't that funny?"

I pause, then decide on what I think is true. "Don't do it to her, Annie," I say. Then I go find my mother.

"J.T.," I say, "I need to take my mother home."

"Is she all right?"

"Just do me a favor. Tell Georgia we left and she's not invited over to the house today. Can you do that?"

"What happened?"

"Just do it, J.T."

"Are you OK?" he asks.

"Listen," I say, "I might not be OK, but right

now I've got too much going on to worry about you, all right? I'm sorry, but I don't think this is going to work out the way you want it to...at least not right now."

J.T. steps back. "And you think you know the way I want this to work out?"

I shrug. His face is angry, yet kind, and I just can't deal with this right now.

"I have to go," I say, turning away. Jessie's in the sandbox. She screams as I grab her and carry her to my mother, who is standing with a group of older Camellias.

"We need to leave," I hiss. "Now."

"I'll get Georgia."

I can see the shadow of disapproval fall over the Camellia faces.

"Georgia's going with J.T."

My mother looks at me quizzically. "Well, ladies, it looks like my daughter needs me for something."

"Sorry, girls," I say. I march us wordlessly to the sedan. Jessie is still screaming when I strap her into the backseat.

"No, mammy. Fish!" she wails. "I wanted fish!"

"Sarah, what is this about?"

"Mom, we'll talk about it at the house."

My mother purses her painted lips and glares out the window.

"I don't appreciate being treated this way."

"Not talking in front of Jessie, Mom."

I get us home in fifteen minutes. Jessie is still sniffling, but after I cheat all laws of good motherhood and set her up with a bowl of chocolate pudding and a cartoon movie, she settles down.

When I find Mom, she's on the porch. She's already poured herself a large drink.

"Do you want to tell me," she says lividly, "what this is about?"

"So I was talking to Annie."

"Annie Mitchell? She's grown up quite nicely, hasn't she?"

"She says Georgia's been living here for months."

"Two nice children," my mother continues, "and that nice husband of hers."

"While Daddy was alive, Mom."

"It's nice that she got married, isn't it?"

"What kind of fucked up things were happening here? How was Daddy supposed to live here with the two of you carrying on?"

"There was no carrying on, Sarah," Mom says calmly. "And don't swear. It doesn't become you. Besides, darling, the person we really should be talking about out here is you."

"Excuse me? *What?* What about me?"

I watch her, my head boiling, as she settles onto the sofa.

"Sit."

"No."

She nods, crossing her legs. "All right. Well, to start, what are you doing, thinking you can raise that child alone?"

"Mom, I've been perfectly fine on my own for a long time."

"You're not fine. That's ridiculous. You've never been fine. Do you know how worried your father was about you?"

"What do you mean?"

" 'My little lost Sarah,' he used to say. 'What's going to happen to Sarah?' "

"That's not fair," I say. "Anyway, I don't believe you."

"Believe what you want," she said, emitting a sharp sigh. "You're a mess. A total mess."

I turn and look at the river. It really is amazing here, after living in the city. You can see the boats for miles.

"You know what, Mom? Just because I'm not the perfect grown-up Camellia doesn't mean I'm a mess."

"Oh, the Camellias. Of course. You're *so* much better than us. We've noticed."

"I bet you have. I bet you've noticed every screwup I've ever had and decided it's because I don't properly understand the Camellia Code."

"Well, it is a question, isn't it? Why you can't hang in. What did happen with Max, anyway? You wouldn't tell us. And the others? And where exactly is Jessie's daddy? And why for the love of Jesus can't you just give J.T. a chance?"

I am so exasperated, I just want to throw something. Am I too old to throw a glass? How about a flowerpot?

"I don't know, Mom. I don't know why these things don't work out. They just don't. All I know is that when the shit hits the fan, y'alls little codes and rules are pretty damned useless."

"Maybe you're relying on them to tell you the wrong things."

I shake my head. "That's great, Mom. Convenient answer. Anyway, you know what? I can't believe I'm letting you attack me right now, when you're the one with the guilty conscience."

"Excuse me?"

"Everyone knows about this thing with Georgia," I say. "Everyone knows it's been going on behind Daddy's back. Oh, excuse me—while he was in the damned room."

"That's not true."

"Is that why he killed himself? Huh? Because he couldn't stand seeing you with Georgia?"

Mom sighs and looks at me square. "Sarah."

"Did he? It's just this feeling I have that you're not telling me everything. What is it? What is the truth?"

"Georgia has been around me, yes."

"And you couldn't just divorce him, like any normal lesbian?"

My mother flinches. I know she hates the word. I dig in. "That's what you are when you love another woman, Mom," I say. "Get used to it. You're a lesbian."

"Your father shot himself," she says quietly, "because he was dying."

Oh, God.

Goddamn.

"What?" I whisper.

"He had a stroke. The man could barely move. He couldn't even go to the bathroom by himself."

"Dad?" My eyes start to sting. I can't see.

"I told Georgia because I couldn't stand it. So she was helping."

"Oh, God." I sit down next to her and put my head in my hands, pulling at my hair. "Why didn't you *tell* us?"

"He didn't want me to," she says. "He didn't want anyone to feel bad for him."

"I just wish—"

"I know," she says.

We sit for a few minutes in silence. I look at the ripe marsh again, at the dull silver water sliding through the grass. That water comes all the way from the other end of the world. It's born on an iceberg in Antarctica or Greenland. Does it ever fully disappear? Or does it spend eternity evaporating and freezing and pouring over itself to get here, just to turn right around at the blink of the tide and go back to where it came from again?

"Anyway," my mother finally says, "about the Camellias."

"I know," I say. "Commit to J.T. Give it a chance."

"I don't care if you do or don't. And the Camellias don't care if you do or don't. We're not evil, Sarah. We're a little old-fashioned, maybe. But really, what all those rules are about is tradition. You think tradition is silly. I know you do."

I shrug. I am not sure of anything anymore. "Maybe."

"But do you ever think," my mother says, putting her arm around me, "that you might be able to use a little tradition?"

I grit my teeth. If there is one thing I'm not in the mood for right now, it's a lecture about the Camellias. And I still hate girl hugs.

"It's not all bad, you know."

"Well, what about Georgia?" I say. "What do the soldiers of supportive tradition have to say about her?"

"The Camellias are glad that she's happy."

"Right."

"Actually, that brings up a good point. About Georgia, I mean."

"So you're not lovers. God, I'm sorry, Mom. So sorry. I'm a big, fat idiot, like everyone else in town. See? You can't take the Camellia out of me. I guess I was raised right."

"Sarah," she says, "we're not lovers now, but I..." She falters.

"What?" I say.

"There's nothing wrong with me. I'm not crazy. But I know what I want. I loved your father, but...Georgia." She crosses her arms over her chest. "I want her. To be with her. Always."

I blink. I am a little surprised at how not surprised I am.

"You sure, Mom?"

My mother smiles sadly. "I'm pretty sure."

"Pretty sure? Because you know we'll all be OK with it. We love Georgia. But people will talk. Especially when you move to town."

"We're not moving to town, Sarah." My mother looks at me, then looks away. Her expression is familiar. I've seen it before on my sister, on my mother, on me. "So, *lesbian*." She gives a long sigh. "Yes. I suppose that is the word for what I am."

"It's a good word," I say. "I like it."

"Love changes all the time," my mother says, wiping tears from her eyes. "I've been in it for years."

I put my head on her shoulder.

"Same here, Mom," I say. "Me too."

At eight sharp, the doorbell rings.

J.T. and Georgia arrive together. They don't know why they've been called after the crazy way we've been acting today, but they both seem happy enough to be here and don't ask questions. Georgia heads to the kitchen and J.T. pins me against the wall for a kiss. It's our first, and it is delicious.

"Hey," he says.

"Sorry about the fish fry."

"Hush."

"Mom's cooking," I say.

"Are you helping her?" J.T. asks.

"There's something you should know," I say. "Not only do I not do church but I can't cook."

"Fair enough," J.T. says, reluctantly pulling away from me. He picks up Jessie and puts her on his hip. She beams. "I'm not half bad at it, anyway."

"Good," I say.

After dinner, we leave the dirty dishes on the table and put J.T.'s favorite, Willie Nelson, on Dad's old record player. Georgia, Jessie, and Mom sway together, while J.T. takes me in his arms and starts to Lindy.

"Look at that, Liza," Georgia says. "The boy can dance."

"Oh, sure," he says. "My great-aunt was a Camellia."

"Well, damn it all to hell," Georgia says.

We dance to the music. Jessie claps her hands and jumps, and I twist and step-ball-step and think about the truth. That next week I'll more likely than not take Jessie on an airplane away from here. That Mom will never feel comfortable publicly being Georgia's lover. That J.T. and I will probably never be anything: my cynicism will cut him; his good nature and faith will wear me down. And then there's the truth beyond that, sitting like an old rock under green creek water: none of these things matter. Right now, in this moment, we have love. We have it in the sound of my daughter's laughter, in Mom's and Georgia's locked fingers, in the warm pressure of J.T.'s hand. It will leave, and it will come again, and when it does I'll give up everything and take it. Just like an addict. Like dry grass in new rain. It's not something I'm proud of, necessarily. Then again, maybe I am.

That's it, I guess. That's all I know.

ACKNOWLEDGMENTS

I would like to thank my fifth-grade English teacher, Dorothy Rhett, who told me I was a writer.

Thanks to my family for agreeing with her.

Thanks to Rob McQuilkin, the best agent a girl could ever hope for, and to my wise and glamorous editor, Judith Clain.

Thanks to everyone at Little, Brown. I am so proud to live in your house.

Thanks to the MacDowell Colony.

Finally, thanks to the people who, by offering their advice and constant friendship, helped me to write this book. This list includes but is not limited to: Grady Hendrix and Amanda Cohen, Maddy and Jason Hanley, Rachel Levin and Josh Richter, Liz and Neal Dessouky, Chuck and Sally Greer, Anne Krumme, Matt Krumme, Farley Urmston, Michael Barrientos, Aaron Stern, Eugenia Payne, Andrea Vazzano,

Molly Lindley, Tom Parker, Jonny Segura, Jon Dee, and Rosalie, Bill, Richard, and Heather Crouch.

I think every day about how lucky I am, and I want to find some way to show you how much your support and love mean to me. But even if I stretched my left arm west to reach the lights of Tokyo, and my right arm east to graze the coast of Papua New Guinea—toes and head straining toward the icy poles—it wouldn't work. I still wouldn't be able to explain.

ABOUT THE AUTHOR

Katie Crouch grew up in Charleston, South Carolina, and studied writing at Brown and Columbia Universities. She lives in San Francisco.